I Am a Child of God

Cort Curtis

Published by Cort Curtis, Ph.D., 2023.

This is a work of fiction. Similarities to real people, places, or events are entirely coincidental.

I AM A CHILD OF GOD

First edition. September 3, 2023.

ISBN: 979-8223884156

Written by Cort Curtis.

Also by Cort Curtis

All You Need Is Love
I Am a Child of God

Table of Contents

To all the young souls embarking on their journey of faith—may these tales light your way and fill your heart with endless joy and wisdom.

To the parents, grandparents, aunts, uncles, and guardians who turn the pages of this book with love in their hands and prayer in their hearts—may you find as much inspiration in reading these tales as your little ones do in hearing them.

And finally, to the eternal Child of God in each of us—never stop seeking, learning, and loving.

With blessings and love,

Cort

The Little Seed That Became Bread of Life

ONCE UPON A TIME IN the whimsical land of Harvestville, a small seed lay buried deep in the soil. Unlike its neighbors—rose seeds, corn seeds, and sunflower seeds—the little seed was uncertain about what it would become. The neighboring seeds always boasted about their glorious futures.

"I'm going to be the most beautiful rose, and people will admire me all day!" said the rose seed.

"I'll be a tall stalk of corn, feeding families far and wide," declared the corn seed.

"I'll be a radiant sunflower, and I'll reach high into the sky to catch the sun's light," said the sunflower seed proudly.

But the little seed felt quite unremarkable. "What good can I be?" it thought.

Days turned into weeks, and weeks turned into months. The rose seed grew into a lovely rose bush, the corn seed into a robust cornstalk, and the sunflower seed into a dazzling sunflower that touched the sky. Yet, the little seed remained buried, feeling lonelier and less significant than ever before.

However, its destiny was yet to unfold. One day, gentle hands unearthed it and planted it into rich, nourishing soil.

"You are special," whispered the wind.

"You are important," sang the birds.

"You have a purpose," hummed the earth.

1

With newfound hope, the little seed began to grow. It didn't grow into a stunning rose or a tall stalk of corn or a dazzling sunflower. It grew into a humble wheat plant.

Farmers harvested it and ground it into flour. The flour was then made into bread. The bread wasn't glamorous, but it was vital. It sat in the center of tables, uniting families. It filled empty stomachs, nourishing people from the inside out.

One day, a wise old man walked into Harvestville holding a staff. He had heard tales of the little seed that had turned into the 'Bread of Life.'

"I've traveled far and wide, and I've seen many wonders," said the wise man. "But there's something extraordinary about the bread made from this wheat plant. It's like it feeds the soul."

The wise man broke the bread and shared it with everyone in Harvestville. And as they ate, a magical thing happened. They felt their worries lighten, their spirits soar, and their hearts fill with an unspeakable joy.

"This bread is like no other," said the wise man. "Whoever partakes of it feels love and contentment. It is the bread of life; whoever comes to it shall not hunger, and whoever believes in its magic shall never thirst."

From that day on, the little seed that had once felt so unremarkable became the most treasured plant in all of Harvestville. It didn't just feed the body; it fed the soul. And so, everyone lived happily and heartily ever after.

And that, dear friends, is how the little seed became the Bread of Life.

"I am the bread of life; whoever comes to me shall not hunger, and whoever believes in me shall never thirst."

Luma, the Light of the Forest

IN THE HEART OF VERDANT Forest, where the sun seldom touched the ground, lived magical creatures, big and small. Yet, the forest was shadowed by an everlasting darkness that made it difficult for the creatures to find their way.

Among these creatures was Luma, a small firefly with an unusually bright glow. Unlike other fireflies that flickered and dimmed, Luma's light never waned.

"I am the light of the forest," Luma would often say, "and those who follow me shall not walk in darkness."

For some, this was hard to believe. In a world so overshadowed, how could one little firefly make a difference?

"I'll stick to my lantern," said Sammy the Snail, carrying a tiny light that barely pierced the dark.

"I have my echo to guide me," boasted Tina the Bat, relying on sound rather than sight.

But Oliver the Owl saw something different in Luma. "May I follow you, Luma?" asked Oliver. "This darkness has made it difficult for me to find food for my little ones."

"Of course, Oliver," Luma answered. "When you follow the light, the path becomes clear."

As Oliver followed Luma, they found plenty. With Luma's guiding light, Oliver could spot fruits and small critters easily. His family would not go hungry that night.

Soon, word spread about Luma's gift. As more creatures began to follow her, they discovered they could see the beauty of the forest for the first time. They saw the colors of the flowers, the shapes of the leaves, and even the tiny dewdrops that sparkled like gems.

As they continued to follow Luma, another miracle unfolded: the creatures themselves started to glow. Not as brightly as Luma, but enough to illuminate their way.

"Incredible," said Emily the Sparrow. "I can now find my way back to my nest."

"It's a miracle," said Freddie the Frog. "I've never felt so alive."

And so, the once dark forest became a place of light and life. The creatures who followed Luma found their way, and more importantly, they found their purpose.

Luma would often say, "I am the light of the world; he who follows me will not walk in darkness, but will have the light of life."

And so, every creature in Verdant Forest found not just light but also the light of life. Luma's light had made all the difference, turning a somber forest into a sanctuary of hope and life.

"I am the light of the world; he who follows me will not walk in darkness, but will have the light of life."

The Enchanted Doorway of Meadowgrove

IN A SECLUDED CORNER of the land of Meadowgrove, known for its lush fields and crystal-clear rivers, stood an ancient, enchanted doorway. Unlike other doors, this one stood alone, framed by vines and wildflowers, with no walls on either side. It was a mystery, a subject of local legends and children's bedtime stories.

The doorway was known to be special because of an old inscription that read, "I am the door; if anyone enters by me, he will be saved and will go in and out and find pasture."

In Meadowgrove, lives weren't always easy. Crops sometimes failed, rivers flooded, and the winter could be particularly harsh. Yet, the enchanted doorway stood as a symbol of hope and promise, though no one had ever dared to step through it.

Except for young Timmy, a shepherd boy who had heard the tales but never thought much of them. He was more concerned about his flock of sheep, who were struggling to find pasture in the ongoing drought.

One particularly tough day, as Timmy saw his sheep grow weaker from the lack of food, he thought about the mysterious doorway. "Could it be true?" he wondered. "Could the doorway lead to a place of abundant pasture?"

Timmy decided it was worth the risk. He led his sheep toward the doorway, his heart pounding with both fear and excitement. As they approached, the door seemed to shimmer, as if beckoning them closer.

With a deep breath, Timmy stepped through the doorway, his sheep following closely behind.

As they crossed the threshold, they found themselves in an entirely different place—a place of endless meadows, blooming flowers, and sparkling streams. The sheep immediately began to graze on the lush grass, their spirits lifting with every mouthful.

Timmy was amazed. The old inscription was true: "I am the door; if anyone enters by me, he will be saved and will go in and out and find pasture."

For weeks, Timmy and his sheep stayed in this magical land. They grew strong and healthy, their wool thickening, and their eyes brightening. But Timmy remembered his home and the people of Meadowgrove, who needed to know about this place of salvation.

Timmy led his sheep back through the enchanted doorway to Meadowgrove. The villagers were amazed at the transformation of his once frail flock.

"Where did you find such lush pasture?" they asked.

"It's through the enchanted doorway," Timmy explained. "It's true what the inscription says. If anyone enters by it, they will be saved and find pasture."

From that day on, the people of Meadowgrove would occasionally step through the enchanted doorway, each time returning revitalized and hopeful, carrying stories of a place where dreams were possible and hopes were realized.

And so, the enchanted doorway stood, no longer just a subject of myths and legends, but a beacon of hope and promise for all who were in need.

"I am the door; if anyone enters by me, he will be saved and will go in and out and find pasture."

Shep, the Good Shepherd of Stony Hills

IN A QUAINT VILLAGE named Stony Hills, surrounded by rugged mountains and vast meadows, lived Shep, a shepherd known far and wide for his kindness and bravery. His flock of sheep was the healthiest and happiest in all the land. And while other shepherds used their staffs only for herding, Shep used his to draw circles in the soil, teaching the young villagers how to count, write, and even dream.

The secret to Shep's successful flock was his unending devotion. He would always say, "I am the good shepherd; the good shepherd lays down his life for the sheep."

Many in Stony Hills found it hard to understand Shep's dedication. "Why risk your life for mere sheep?" they would ask.

But Shep knew something they did not. He knew each of his sheep by name, and he knew that caring for his flock was his life's calling.

One ominous night, a wolf—a creature of pure dread with sharp teeth and a thirst for chaos—entered the meadows of Stony Hills. The other shepherds, upon hearing its howl, quickly locked themselves inside their homes, leaving their flocks to fend for themselves.

Not Shep. Grasping his staff, he ventured into the dark, guided only by the light of the moon and the flicker of his lantern.

As he reached his flock, he found the wolf staring intently at Bella, his oldest and wisest ewe. But before the wolf could make its move, Shep stepped between them.

The wolf growled, its eyes locked onto Shep.

"I am the good shepherd," said Shep, his voice unwavering. "And a good shepherd lays down his life for his sheep. Leave now, and I won't harm you. Stay, and you'll find that even a good shepherd can fight."

For a moment, the air was thick with tension. Then, as if understanding the depth of Shep's resolve, the wolf turned and retreated into the dark forest, never to be seen in Stony Hills again.

When the villagers learned of Shep's bravery, they realized the truth in his words. A good shepherd does lay down his life for his sheep, not just in facing physical dangers, but in the love, care, and devotion he provides every day.

From that day forward, Shep's reputation grew beyond Stony Hills. Parents told their children about the brave and kind shepherd who faced a wolf and won. And as for his flock, they lived long, healthy lives, each one bearing a patch of wool brighter than the rest—a sign, the villagers said, that they were truly loved.

"I am the good shepherd; the good shepherd lays down his life for the sheep.'

Elyra and the Blossom of Eternal Spring

IN A DISTANT REALM, far beyond the mountains and across the enchanted seas, there was a magical tree known as the Tree of Eternal Spring. It was a tree unlike any other; its leaves shimmered with colors unknown to the human eye, and its blossoms were said to hold the power of life itself.

However, the tree had lost its vibrant hues over time, and the realm was threatened by a never-ending winter. Without the tree's power, life couldn't be sustained.

Elyra, a young and courageous girl, decided to undertake the perilous journey to find the Tree of Eternal Spring and restore it. "I am the resurrection and the life," she heard whispered through the winds as she embarked on her quest, "he who believes in me, though he die, yet shall he live."

After days of walking through treacherous terrain and dark forests, Elyra finally reached the dying tree. Its leaves were withered, and its blossoms were nowhere to be found.

She took a deep breath, reached into her satchel, and pulled out a tiny seed she'd been carrying since the start of her journey—a seed given to her by her grandmother, who had whispered, "Believe in the promise of renewal, and you shall bring life where there is none."

With faith in her heart, Elyra planted the seed at the base of the Tree of Eternal Spring, and softly whispered, "I believe."

As if responding to her faith, the seed began to glow. A pulse of radiant energy surged from it, connecting with the roots of the tree. Before her eyes, the Tree of Eternal Spring began to regain its colors;

blossoms sprouted, and a wave of warmth spread across the realm, pushing back the endless winter.

Suddenly, a single, magnificent blossom detached from a branch and floated gently towards Elyra. It was the Blossom of Eternal Spring—proof that life had been restored.

Elyra carried the blossom back to her village, where the people were in awe of its beauty and the story of the restored Tree of Eternal Spring. From that day on, the Blossom of Eternal Spring stood as a symbol of undying faith and life eternal in the heart of the village.

As for Elyra, she became known as the one who believed in the promise of resurrection and life. And it was said that whoever believed in the tale, though they might face hardships, would find a way to live again—refreshed, renewed, and full of life.

"I am the resurrection and the life; he who believes in me, though he die, yet shall he live."

The Journey of Arlo, the True Guide of Eldoria

IN THE MAGICAL KINGDOM of Eldoria, where towering castles were surrounded by blooming gardens, there was an age-old legend. The legend spoke of the mystical Pathway of Wisdom that led to the dwelling of the Great Father, the supreme guardian of the land's magic and prosperity.

However, the pathway was filled with illusions, mazes, and riddles that no one could solve. Many tried to traverse it, seeking the wisdom and blessings of the Great Father, but they all returned empty-handed, lost in the web of illusions.

Among the wise elders and fearless knights was Arlo, a humble gardener who had a deep understanding of both the earth and the sky. Arlo often said, "I am the way, and the truth, and the life; no one comes to the Father, but by me."

Many chuckled at his claim. "How can a gardener be the guide to the Pathway of Wisdom?" they wondered. But Arlo had a secret; he had spent years studying ancient scrolls and deciphering the language of the natural world.

Determined to prove that he was indeed the true guide, Arlo invited anyone who wished to reach the Great Father to join him on a journey through the mystical pathway.

A group of brave souls—knights, scholars, and even common folk—joined him. As they stepped onto the Pathway of Wisdom, they were immediately engulfed by illusions and mazes that seemed to shift with every step they took.

However, Arlo remained focused. He would touch a seemingly random stone, or hum a specific tune, and the illusions would dissipate, revealing the true path ahead.

Whenever they reached a fork in the road, Arlo would pause and say, "I am the way." And the correct path would magically become clear.

Whenever they encountered a riddle or enigma, he would muse, "I am the truth." And the answer would reveal itself.

Whenever the travelers grew tired or lost hope, he would reassure them, "I am the life." And a newfound energy would invigorate them.

Finally, the group arrived at the dwelling of the Great Father. Amazed by Arlo's wisdom and guidance, the Great Father bestowed his blessings upon the land, ensuring prosperity and peace for generations to come.

The travelers returned to Eldoria as heroes, their hearts and minds enlightened. Arlo, once a humble gardener, became known as the True Guide of Eldoria, revered for his wisdom and humility.

And so, the saying was forever etched in the history of Eldoria: "I am the way, and the truth, and the life; no one comes to the Father, but by me."

"I am the way, and the truth, and the life; no one comes to the Father, but by me."

The Enchanted Vine of Veritas Valley

IN THE TRANQUIL LANDS of Veritas Valley, life was fruitful and serene, thanks to an ancient, enchanted vine known as Vita. This magical vine was no ordinary plant; it was the lifeblood of the valley, and from its branches grew fruits of wisdom, joy, and prosperity.

Everyone in the valley tended to the vine, but none as much as Elara, a young gardener who had an almost mystical connection with Vita. Elara would often say, "I am the vine; you are the branches. Whoever abides in me and I in him, he it is that bears much fruit, for apart from me you can do nothing."

Over time, the people grew complacent and began to take the vine for granted. They assumed that the magical fruits would always be abundant, without any need for care or nurturing.

Elara noticed the vine starting to wither and felt a deep sense of responsibility to save it. She tried to warn the villagers, but her words fell on deaf ears. They had become so accustomed to the vine's gifts that they'd forgotten its need for nurture and love.

Knowing she had to act, Elara started spending her days and nights caring for Vita, pruning its branches, speaking words of encouragement, and even singing lullabies to the vine. Her dedication began to bear fruit—literally.

New branches sprouted, laden with even more magical fruits than before. These fruits were extraordinary, with the power to heal, rejuvenate, and even inspire those who consumed them.

When the villagers tasted the new fruits, they were amazed. The flavors were unlike anything they had ever experienced, and the sense of wellness and vitality that washed over them was profound.

The village elders approached Elara and asked her how she had managed to revive the vine.

"It's simple," she said. "This vine—Vita—is our source of life. But it too needs life from us. We are its branches, and if we abide in it, the fruits we bear will be plentiful. Remember, apart from it, we can do nothing."

From then on, the people of Veritas Valley took turns caring for the vine, learning the arts of pruning, watering, and even talking to it, all under Elara's guidance.

The vine continued to flourish, its branches extending throughout the valley, providing magical fruits for all. And it was said that as long as the people remembered their role as the vine's branches, Veritas Valley would remain a place of endless bounty and eternal peace.

"I am the vine; you are the branches. Whoever abides in me and I in him, he it is that bears much fruit, for apart from me you can do nothing."

Orion, Keeper of Eternal Time

IN THE MYSTICAL REALM of Tempora, where time ebbed and flowed like the tides of an eternal ocean, lived Orion, the Keeper of Eternal Time. He was not merely a guardian; he was time itself.

"I am the Alpha and the Omega, the first and the last, the beginning and the end," he would often proclaim, his voice echoing through the layers of past, present, and future.

Orion was responsible for maintaining the balance of time in Tempora. With his celestial staff, he could open gates to the past and future, but only when absolutely necessary. For meddling with time was a dangerous affair.

However, balance was disrupted when a rogue sorcerer named Vortex sought to control time for his own gains. He planned to manipulate the past to alter the present, striving for eternal dominion over Tempora.

Learning of Vortex's intentions, Orion realized that he had to act. Yet, he also knew that intervening directly would risk fracturing the timelines irreparably.

So, instead, Orion chose a different path. He opened a gate to the distant past, where he met young Elara, a brave girl with a curious heart. Sharing only what was necessary, Orion provided Elara with the Seed of Continuity, a magical seed that could restore balance to Tempora if planted at the very center of the realm.

Confused but trusting, Elara undertook the quest. She navigated treacherous terrains, battled ferocious beasts, and solved intricate puzzles to reach the center of Tempora, not knowing that her actions were carving a new timeline—one where Vortex never rose to power.

When she planted the Seed of Continuity, the timelines adjusted, unraveling Vortex's tampering and restoring balance to Tempora. As the seed sprouted, it formed a cosmic tree, its branches and roots stretching into all moments of time.

Orion, sensing the restoration of balance, appeared before Elara to thank her.

"But how does a simple seed hold such power?" she asked.

Smiling, Orion replied, "Just as I am the beginning and the end, this seed is the embodiment of continuity and eternal balance. It was the first seed to ever exist and it will be the last to ever perish. It exists in every moment, ensuring the harmony of time."

Elara returned to her own time, forever cherishing the secret of her extraordinary journey. And so, Tempora remained a realm of balanced time, ever flowing yet eternally stable, watched over by Orion, the Keeper who was both the first and the last, the Alpha and the Omega.

"I am the Alpha and the Omega, the first and the last, the beginning and the end."

The Humble Kingdom of Celestia's Sky

IN A KINGDOM ABOVE the clouds, called Celestia, where everyone could fly, there lived a young boy named Finn who was different. Unlike the others, Finn couldn't fly. No matter how hard he tried to flutter his wings, he remained grounded.

While others soared through the open skies, exploring the celestial wonders and gathering stardust, Finn spent his time reading ancient scriptures and listening to the tales of wise elders. Among these scriptures was a phrase he took to heart: "Blessed are the poor in spirit, for theirs is the kingdom of heaven."

Finn had always considered his inability to fly a lack in spirit, but the phrase gave him hope. If even the 'poor in spirit' could have a place in the kingdom of heaven, then surely he had a place in Celestia.

Soon, the kingdom faced a dire crisis. A dark cloud enveloped Celestia, threatening to dim its eternal light. The people tried to disperse the cloud by flying through it, but it was too thick and would not budge.

Distraught, the King of Celestia called a council meeting. "How can we disperse this ominous cloud?" he asked.

No one had an answer, except for Finn. "Your Majesty," he began hesitantly, "I have spent my days studying the ancient scriptures. They speak of the 'Light of Humility' that can only be ignited by those who are poor in spirit. I believe I can summon this light."

The King looked at Finn, then at his council, and finally said, "We have tried everything else. Let Finn try."

With the kingdom's gaze upon him, Finn stood before the dark cloud. He closed his eyes and thought of his life—his struggles, his grounded existence, and his humble spirit. As he held the scripture close to his heart, he whispered, "Blessed are the poor in spirit, for theirs is the kingdom of heaven."

Suddenly, a soft light emanated from within him, growing brighter and brighter, until it shot up into the sky and pierced through the dark cloud. The cloud dispersed, revealing the clear sky and celestial wonders once again.

From that day forth, Finn became a beacon of hope and wisdom in Celestia. Though he never gained the ability to fly, he taught the people that one didn't need wings to soar, that being poor in spirit was not a curse but a blessing, a different kind of richness that held its own place in the kingdom of heaven—or in his case, the kingdom of Celestia.

"Blessed are the poor in spirit, for theirs is the kingdom of heaven."

The Garden of Solace: A Tale of Eternal Blossoms

IN THE MAGICAL REALM of Elysia, a beautiful garden known as the Garden of Solace stood as a sanctuary for those seeking comfort and peace. This was no ordinary garden; it was a living testament to the powerful mantra: "Blessed are those who mourn, for they shall be comforted."

Everyone in Elysia knew that when you felt sorrow, the Garden of Solace was the place to go. The flowers that grew there had a magical quality; they absorbed the sorrow of anyone who visited, transforming their tears into breathtaking blossoms.

A young girl named Lily often found solace in the garden. Her life had been marred by tragedy, having lost both of her parents at a young age. Lily would sit by her favorite patch of violet blooms, her tears watering the soil as her sorrow turned into magnificent flowers.

One day, the realm of Elysia was threatened by a dark force, a shadow that crept slowly across the land, swallowing light and joy. The Elders, wise but frail, knew of only one way to combat this darkness—a bouquet of Eternal Blossoms from the Garden of Solace, formed from the most potent tears.

However, plucking these flowers was not an easy task. The Eternal Blossoms would only reveal themselves to one who had experienced deep sorrow but also had the resilience to hold onto hope.

The Elders believed Lily was the one who could do it. With a heavy heart but a glimmer of hope, she entered the garden, knelt by her violet blooms, and began to weep. As her tears touched the soil, a radiant light erupted from the ground, revealing the mesmerizing Eternal Blossoms.

Holding the bouquet carefully, Lily approached the creeping shadow. She felt an overwhelming sense of sorrow emanate from it, as if it, too, was mourning. With a deep breath, Lily placed the bouquet of Eternal Blossoms into the heart of the shadow.

For a moment, everything was still. Then, the bouquet absorbed the shadow's sorrow, glowing brighter and brighter until the shadow dispersed, vanquished by its own mournful essence, now transformed into light.

From that day on, Lily became a symbol of resilience and hope in Elysia. She continued to visit the Garden of Solace, but now she went not just to find comfort but also to offer it to others. She often told them, "Blessed are those who mourn, for in this garden, you shall find comfort."

And so, the Garden of Solace remained a sanctuary for all, its Eternal Blossoms a testament to the transformative power of sorrow and the enduring comfort it could bring.

"Blessed are those who mourn, for they shall be comforted."

The Quest for the Pure Spring: A Tale of Righteous Longing

IN A KINGDOM DIVIDED by injustice and strife, there was a tale whispered in hushed tones—a tale of a Pure Spring that could quench the deepest thirst for righteousness. The water of this spring, it was said, granted wisdom and courage to uphold justice.

Tessa, a young woman from a humble background, had heard this tale from her grandmother. She believed in it wholeheartedly and often declared, "Blessed are those who hunger and thirst for righteousness, for they shall be satisfied."

Tessa's passion for justice was not just limited to words. She was an active member of her community, standing against oppression and inequality wherever she saw it. However, she soon realized that the problems were too vast for one person to handle. What she needed was the wisdom and courage that the Pure Spring could offer.

One day, she decided she could no longer wait. She packed her belongings and embarked on a quest to find the legendary spring. Her journey was fraught with challenges—treacherous landscapes, menacing creatures, and puzzles that tested her wit and courage.

Days turned into weeks, and weeks into months. Tessa faced each obstacle with an unwavering resolve, her thirst for righteousness urging her on. Finally, after a year-long quest, she arrived at a serene clearing where the Pure Spring sparkled under the moonlight.

As she knelt down to drink, a guardian spirit of the spring appeared. "Why do you seek the waters of this spring?" it asked.

"I hunger and thirst for righteousness," Tessa replied, her voice filled with sincerity. "I seek to bring justice to my kingdom, and I believe these waters will grant me the wisdom and courage to do so."

The guardian spirit, moved by her earnestness, allowed her to drink from the spring. As Tessa took a sip, she felt an overwhelming sense of clarity and strength wash over her.

Upon her return, Tessa found her kingdom in worse shape than she had left it. But now, she was not the same young woman who had embarked on the quest; she was stronger, wiser, and more courageous.

With her newfound abilities, Tessa led a peaceful revolution, advocating for laws that promoted equality and justice. Slowly but surely, the kingdom began to change. Oppressive policies were repealed, marginalized communities were uplifted, and the once-divided kingdom found a sense of unity.

People came to know of Tessa's quest and the Pure Spring, but what inspired them most was her relentless pursuit of righteousness. They realized that the spring was not just a physical place but a symbol—proof that those who hunger and thirst for righteousness will indeed be satisfied.

Tessa continued to work towards a fairer society, but she often said that her thirst for righteousness was quenched not just by the magical waters, but also by the change she saw in her people.

And so, the kingdom transformed, not by the magic of a mystical spring, but by the insatiable thirst for righteousness that lived in the heart of a humble young woman named Tessa.

"Blessed are those who hunger and thirst for righteousness, for they shall be satisfied."

The Compassionate Keeper: A Tale of Endless Mercy

IN A DISTANT REALM, overshadowed by towering mountains and deep valleys, lay the mystical Forest of Tranquility. This enchanted forest was guarded by Eira, known as the Compassionate Keeper. Eira held a secret key that could unlock the Fountain of Mercy, a magical spring that could bestow forgiveness and compassion to those who sought it.

Eira was no ordinary guardian; she had a heart full of mercy and kindness. She lived by a golden principle: "Blessed are the merciful, for they shall receive mercy."

However, mercy was a rare commodity in the realm. Many were blinded by greed, pride, and jealousy. Among them was Morgana, a sorceress who sought to use the Fountain of Mercy to increase her own power. But the fountain would only reveal itself to the truly merciful, a virtue Morgana knew nothing about.

One fateful day, Morgana conjured a dark spell to find the location of the Fountain of Mercy. The spell backfired, affecting her instead, draining her magic and rendering her vulnerable.

Realizing her own vulnerability, Morgana found herself wandering into the Forest of Tranquility, weak and powerless. Eira discovered her in this pitiable state, and despite knowing of Morgana's dark intentions, she felt compassion for her.

"Even the unkind need kindness," Eira mused, deciding to help Morgana. She used her key to unlock the Fountain of Mercy, allowing Morgana to drink its waters and restore her strength.

"Why would you help me?" asked Morgana, puzzled and somewhat moved by Eira's act of mercy.

"Because mercy is not a sign of weakness, but of strength," Eira replied. "When we give mercy, we open the door to receiving it as well. Today, you needed mercy, and so you have received it. Remember this lesson, Morgana."

Eira's act of kindness had a profound effect on Morgana. She found herself questioning her own motives, her own lack of compassion, and in that moment of reflection, the waters of the Fountain of Mercy began to work their true magic.

Morgana relinquished her pursuit of power and instead chose to study the ways of kindness and mercy under Eira's tutelage. In time, she became a guardian of another enchanted forest, a sister forest to the Forest of Tranquility, known as the Forest of Redemption.

Years later, Eira found herself captured by a malevolent force that sought to control the realm's magical sanctuaries. Just when it seemed that all hope was lost, Morgana arrived, wielding her newfound magic of mercy and compassion to free Eira and defeat the malevolent force.

"Blessed are the merciful, for they shall receive mercy," Morgana whispered as she unlocked Eira's chains, both literally and metaphorically embodying the virtue that she had once ignored.

From then on, the two forests stood as eternal symbols of mercy and redemption, guarded by two compassionate keepers who knew the boundless power of mercy—both given and received.

"Blessed are the merciful, for they shall receive mercy."

Aria: The Pure-Hearted Dreamer

IN THE ETHEREAL LAND of Serenica, where dreams and reality intertwined, lived a young girl named Aria. She was known for her unblemished soul and pure heart, which was as clear as the sparkling lakes of Serenica. Aria had always felt a deep connection to the Divine, and she lived by the belief: "Blessed are the pure in heart, for they shall see God."

Though many in Serenica were enchanted by worldly desires, Aria's focus was always on love, kindness, and wonder. This purity of heart granted her the ability to weave the most magical of dreams—dreams that could heal, uplift, and inspire.

One day, dark clouds formed over Serenica, and the dreams of its people began to twist into nightmares. Dread and sorrow filled the air, and no one knew how to drive the darkness away. The Elder Seers, who were the wisest in the land, were especially perturbed, for their visions had become clouded as well.

Aria, sensing the plight, knew that only a pure-hearted individual could unravel this mystery and restore balance. With the blessing of the Elder Seers, she ventured into the forbidden Dreamweave Forest, believed to be the source of all dreams and nightmares.

In the heart of the forest stood the Mirror of Reflection, a magical mirror said to reveal the true nature of anyone who looked into it. Many had tried, but their impure hearts only produced distorted images.

Aria, standing before the mirror, took a deep breath. As she gazed at her reflection, it shimmered and changed, revealing a divine figure filled with radiant light. For Aria, this was the moment she had always believed in, the moment where her pure heart allowed her to glimpse the Divine.

With tears of joy, Aria spoke to the divine figure, "What must I do to heal my land?"

The figure spoke in melodious tones, "Let the love and purity from your heart flow into Serenica, as a river nourishes a parched land. Your dreams are powerful; dream a dream of healing and love."

Returning to her village, Aria sat under the ancient Dreamweaver Tree, closed her eyes, and began to dream. She dreamt of love overcoming fear, of light dispelling darkness, and of joy triumphing over sorrow.

Slowly, the darkness that had enveloped Serenica began to lift. The people's nightmares turned into dreams of hope and inspiration. Even the Elder Seers found their visions clear once more. Serenica had been healed, all through the purity and love that flowed from Aria's heart.

From that day forward, Aria became known as the Pure-Hearted Dreamer. She continued to inspire and uplift her community, always reminding them, "Blessed are the pure in heart, for not only shall they see God, but they shall also bring a piece of that divinity back to the world."

And so, in the magical land of Serenica, purity of heart was forever celebrated as the greatest of virtues, a window to the Divine, and a pathway to healing.

"Blessed are the pure in heart, for they shall see God."

Elian, the Peacemaker: A Tale of Two Villages

ONCE UPON A TIME, TWO small villages—Lumora and Valeria—sat on opposite sides of a wide river. Despite their close proximity, the villagers never interacted due to an age-old feud. While the exact reason for the animosity was lost in time, the division remained, sustained by suspicion and mistrust.

In the middle of the two villages was a small island where a young man named Elian lived. Elian was unlike any other; he was known for his wisdom, kindness, and above all, his strong desire for peace. He believed with all his heart: "Blessed are the peacemakers, for they shall be called sons of God."

Elian could not bear to see the animosity between the two villages and knew something must be done to reconcile them. But how could he, a single individual, bridge the gap that had lasted for generations?

After much contemplation, Elian crafted a brilliant plan. He planted two unique trees on his island—Lumora Blossoms and Valeria Pines. Over the years, he tenderly nurtured them until they grew tall and splendid, visible from both villages.

Then, Elian sent messages to both villages, inviting their leaders to his island for a feast. Both leaders were curious and intrigued, so they accepted his invitation, albeit cautiously. Upon arriving, they were astonished by the beauty of the Lumora Blossoms and Valeria Pines.

Elian welcomed them warmly, setting a table beneath the trees he had grown. During the feast, he spoke of peace, unity, and the potential prosperity that could come from collaboration. He pointed to the Lumora Blossoms and Valeria Pines, saying, "Just as these trees have grown and thrived together on this small island, so can Lumora and Valeria flourish through unity."

The village leaders were moved by Elian's words and the visual testimony of the thriving trees. Yet, old wounds and suspicions still lingered.

Seeing this, Elian took a bold step. He mixed the seeds of the Lumora Blossoms and Valeria Pines and handed them to each leader. "Plant these in your villages. If they can coexist on the same soil, why can't you?"

Overcome by the simplicity and truth of Elian's actions, the leaders agreed to take the first steps toward reconciliation. They returned to their villages and planted the mixed seeds, which, in time, grew into lush groves, standing as constant reminders of the possibility for peace.

News of the peace initiative spread like wildfire. The villagers, inspired by the example set by their leaders and Elian, started to communicate and cooperate for the first time in generations. Trade flourished, friendships were formed, and the river that once divided them became a symbol of unity.

In recognition of his efforts, both villages erected a monument on Elian's island—a statue of him holding a seed in each hand, an eternal symbol of his role as a peacemaker. They began calling him "Elian, Son of God, and Father of Our Unity."

Elian's belief that he could make a difference had indeed changed the course of history for Lumora and Valeria. He stood as a testament to the ancient wisdom: "Blessed are the peacemakers, for they shall be called sons of God."

And so, in the heart of the river that had once divided them, peace blossomed, nurtured by the love and wisdom of a single, determined peacemaker.

"Blessed are the peacemakers, for they shall be called sons of God."

The Brave Sparrow: A Tale of Righteous Valor

IN THE LUSH FOREST of Serenity, where harmony usually reigned, there lived an assortment of creatures, big and small. However, a wave of disharmony had recently swept through the forest due to a decree from Ravena, the mighty raven who claimed to be the queen of the forest.

Ravena had declared that only birds with dark feathers could drink from the Sacred Pool, a natural spring that had magical qualities. This unfair rule left many birds, especially those with colorful feathers, weakened and saddened. In Ravena's eyes, her rule was promoting 'order,' but everyone knew that it was far from righteous.

Among those who found the decree unjust was Skylar, a humble sparrow with brown feathers tinted with hues of gold and gray. Skylar knew the saying: "Blessed are those who are persecuted for righteousness' sake, for theirs is the kingdom of heaven." Inspired by this wisdom, Skylar felt a moral obligation to stand against Ravena's unjust rule.

Despite the risk of facing the wrath of Ravena and her dark-feathered followers, Skylar flew to the Sacred Pool and drank from its waters openly. This act of defiance angered Ravena, who had Skylar captured and brought before her.

"Why do you defy my rule, Skylar? Don't you know the consequences?" Ravena crowed, her voice tinged with disdain.

"I defy it because it is not righteous," replied Skylar, undeterred. "All creatures of this forest have the right to share in its blessings. Your rule divides us, rather than uniting us in harmony."

Enraged, Ravena ordered that Skylar be imprisoned in a cage, suspended from a tall tree. Skylar was isolated, yet not defeated. As the days passed, the other birds started to notice Skylar's courage, and whispers of his bravery spread throughout the forest.

Soon, birds of all feathers began to congregate around the Sacred Pool, defying Ravena's decree. They started singing songs of unity, their collective melody resonating through the woods. The magical qualities of the Sacred Pool seemed to amplify their voices, which reached even the far corners of the forest.

Frustrated and outnumbered, Ravena finally understood that her rule would never stand. Realizing the error of her ways, she ordered Skylar to be released and rescinded her unfair decree.

As Skylar emerged from his cage, he was greeted by a chorus of cheers. While he had been persecuted, his righteousness had illuminated the path for others to follow, exactly as the ancient wisdom had said.

Ravena, deeply moved by the turn of events, found a newfound respect for the laws of righteousness and fairness. She openly admitted her mistake and vowed to rule with justice henceforth.

And so, the Forest of Serenity regained its harmony, all thanks to Skylar's bravery and moral integrity. His courage served as an eternal lesson to all, reinforcing the truth that "Blessed are those who are persecuted for righteousness' sake, for theirs is the kingdom of heaven."

From that moment on, every creature, regardless of their feathers or fur, drank from the Sacred Pool as equals, living in a forest that had become a little more like heaven on Earth.

"Blessed are those who are persecuted for righteousness' sake, for theirs is the kingdom of heaven."

The Story of Luminara: The Lantern of Hope

IN THE FARAWAY VILLAGE of Nocturne, where the night was eternal and stars were the only source of light, lived Luminara—a humble girl known for her glowing heart. She had an inner light that was brighter than any star in the sky, and her good deeds were as numerous as the grains of sand on the shore.

Luminara lived by a sacred principle: "Let your light shine before others, so that they may see your good works and give glory to your Father in heaven." Inspired by this belief, she made lanterns out of starlight and gifted them to her neighbors. These weren't ordinary lanterns; they glowed brighter when carried by those who performed kind deeds.

However, the village was governed by Nightshade, a selfish ruler who hoarded the brightest stars and allowed only a few dim ones to light up the village. Nightshade was wary of Luminara's growing influence and her mysterious lanterns of light.

Unbeknownst to Nightshade, Luminara had discovered a hidden cavern filled with the rarest and brightest of all stars—Heartstars. She decided to craft a special lantern using a Heartstar and place it in the village square. This lantern would be so luminous that it could turn night into day.

Luminara unveiled the Heartstar lantern in the village square and lit it for all to see. The villagers were amazed; its light was so radiant that it illuminated every corner of Nocturne, revealing hidden paths and long-forgotten beauty.

Nightshade, realizing his dim stars paled in comparison to the Heartstar lantern, felt his power waning. Frustrated, he ordered his guards to extinguish the lantern and bring Luminara before him.

"How dare you outshine my stars? Do you wish to make a mockery of my rule?" Nightshade demanded.

"Your Highness, the light is not meant to undermine you, but to uplift everyone," Luminara replied calmly. "It serves as a reminder that goodness and love are the true sources of illumination."

Moved by her courage and the undeniable beauty the Heartstar lantern had brought to the village, Nightshade began to question the purpose of his hoarding and selfishness.

Luminara continued, "If we let our lights shine before others, not to seek praise for ourselves but to inspire good works, we give glory to something greater than us. We create a heaven here in Nocturne."

The room filled with a warmth that even Nightshade could not ignore. He realized the wisdom in Luminara's words and felt his heart change.

Nightshade ordered that all the hoarded stars be distributed among the villagers and declared Luminara's Heartstar lantern as the eternal light of Nocturne. From then on, the village prospered, as every villager was inspired by the radiant light to be kinder and more generous.

Luminara's influence extended beyond just a lantern; she had sparked a change in the hearts of the people, reminding them that light and goodness come from shared acts of kindness.

The Heartstar lantern continued to glow in the village square, a tribute to Luminara and the eternal truth: "Let your light shine before others, so that they may see your good works and give glory to your Father in heaven."

"Let your light shine before others, so that they may see your good works and give glory to your Father in heaven."

Timble: The Mole of His Word

IN THE HEART OF THE Whispering Woods lived Timble, a mole renowned for his honesty and integrity. Timble believed in a simple but powerful principle: "Let your 'yes' be 'yes,' and your 'no' be 'no.'"

This belief was put to the test when the Whispering Woods faced a crisis. A rare Blue Moon was approaching, and legend held that its magic could grant a single wish to the one who found the hidden Moonstone during its cycle. However, the Moonstone could only be touched by the purest of hearts, lest it turn to ordinary rock.

The wise Owl Council decided that someone must be chosen to find the Moonstone. Their eyes turned to Timble, who was known for his straightforwardness and clarity of heart.

"Will you undertake this quest, Timble?" asked Elder Owl, the wisest among them.

"If I say 'yes,' then it shall be a 'yes.' I will find the Moonstone," Timble vowed, knowing well the weight of his words.

As Timble set off on his journey, he encountered various temptations and obstacles. Sly Fox offered him an easier path in exchange for half the Moonstone's powers. Though tempted, Timble remembered his principle and firmly declined, "My 'no' is 'no,' and I shall not waver."

Further along, he met Chatterbird, who offered to spread the word of Timble's bravery if he promised to share the Moonstone's magical gifts. Again, Timble declined, saying, "My mission is clear, and I cannot divert from it. My 'no' must remain a 'no.'"

After many days of searching, Timble finally found the Moonstone glowing beneath the light of the Blue Moon. He touched it, and instead of turning to ordinary rock, the Moonstone sparkled even brighter, recognizing the purity of his heart.

He returned to the Whispering Woods and handed the Moonstone to the Owl Council. "I have fulfilled my 'yes,'" said Timble, his eyes glowing with humble pride.

Elder Owl held the Moonstone high for all to see, then made the community's collective wish—for a shield of protection around the Whispering Woods so that all creatures could live in peace and harmony.

As the wish was granted, the Moonstone dispersed into a thousand twinkling lights, which settled around the forest, creating an invisible shield of protection.

From that day on, Timble became a legend, not just for his bravery or his quest but for the simple, enduring principle he lived by. In a world of complexities and gray areas, Timble stood as a testament to the importance of unwavering honesty and integrity.

In the heart of the Whispering Woods, beneath the ever-protective shield of the Moonstone's magic, creatures young and old were reminded: "Let your 'yes' be 'yes,' and your 'no' be 'no.'"

"Let your yes be yes and your no be no."

The Story of Gemma: The Squirrel Who Understood True Treasure

IN THE DENSE OAKWOOD Forest, where the trees stood tall and the rivers flowed free, lived Gemma the Squirrel. Gemma was unlike any other squirrel in the community. While her friends scurried about collecting acorns, building lavish nests, and boasting about their possessions, Gemma was always more focused on kindness, sharing, and building friendships.

Her friends often chuckled at her, "Gemma, you should be gathering more acorns for the winter! You're falling behind!"

Gemma, however, lived by a principle she once heard from a wandering sage: "Do not lay up for yourselves treasures on earth, where moth and rust destroy and where thieves break in and steal, but lay up for yourselves treasures in heaven, where neither moth nor rust destroys and where thieves do not break in and steal."

One fateful day, a terrible storm swept through Oakwood Forest. Lightning struck, igniting a fire that rapidly spread through the trees. The entire squirrel community was forced to evacuate their nests, leaving behind their cherished acorn collections.

When they returned, they found that their earthly treasures—their acorns and carefully crafted nests—were all destroyed by fire or carried away by the currents of the now-raging river. They were devastated, as they had lost everything they had stored up.

However, Gemma had a different experience. During the fire, the animals she had helped in the past—birds she'd freed from tangled nets, rabbits she'd shared her acorns with, and deer she'd helped find water—came to her aid. Together, they helped Gemma move to a safer part of the forest, far from the destructive flames.

In the aftermath of the disaster, the squirrel community began to understand the wisdom in Gemma's way of life. They realized that their earthly treasures, which they had hoarded so diligently, were impermanent and vulnerable.

Gemma shared what she had left with her community, teaching them to rebuild by focusing on relationships, kindness, and collective well-being. She told them, "It's not about the acorns we gather but the good deeds we scatter. Those are the treasures that no fire can burn, no river can wash away, and no thief can steal."

From that moment on, the squirrels of Oakwood Forest changed their ways. They began to focus less on collecting earthly possessions and more on laying up treasures in 'heaven'—by being kind to one another, sharing what they had, and creating a community where every squirrel looked out for the other.

The forest eventually regrew, stronger and more united than before. And at the heart of this transformation was Gemma, the squirrel who taught everyone that the truest treasures are those stored in heaven—through love, kindness, and a spirit of community.

"Do not lay up for yourselves treasures on earth, where moth and rust destroy and where thieves break in and steal, but lay up for yourselves treasures in heaven, where neither moth nor rust destroys and where thieves do not break in and steal."

The Parable of Faela: The Butterfly With a Heavy Heart

IN THE ENCHANTED MEADOW, a realm of vibrant colors and ever-blooming flowers, lived Faela, a beautiful butterfly with golden wings. Faela had a unique habit: she collected shiny pebbles and stored them in a tiny, hidden cave.

Her fellow butterflies couldn't understand her obsession. "Why waste your time collecting pebbles when you can enjoy the nectar of the flowers and the beauty of the meadow?" they often asked.

Faela shrugged them off, whispering to herself, "For where your treasure is, there your heart will be also." She believed that her collection of glittering pebbles was her true treasure, and so she spent most of her days adding to it.

As time passed, however, Faela began to feel a strange heaviness in her heart. The more pebbles she collected, the less she enjoyed the simple pleasures of the meadow—the aroma of the blossoms, the gentle touch of the breeze, and the sweet songs of the birds. Her heart became so heavy that her once-golden wings began to lose their luster, and she found it increasingly difficult to fly.

Worried, Faela visited Wise Luna, an ancient butterfly known for her insight and wisdom.

After listening to Faela's story, Luna nodded and said, "Faela, you've misunderstood the meaning of treasure. The pebbles you collect might shine, but they're weighing down your heart. They've become your earthly treasure, blinding you to the true treasures around you—love, friendship, and the sheer joy of living."

Faela was taken aback but felt the truth in Luna's words. "What should I do?" she asked, her wings trembling.

Luna smiled gently. "Rediscover your true treasures, Faela. Release the pebbles and lighten your heart. Your heart should be where love, kindness, and joy reside. For where your treasure is, there your heart will be also."

Taking Luna's advice to heart, Faela returned to her hidden cave and, one by one, began to distribute her treasured pebbles among the young butterflies, telling them that the real treasure was not in objects but in relationships and simple pleasures.

As she gave away her last pebble, Faela felt an incredible lightness fill her heart. Her wings regained their golden luster, and she fluttered back to the meadow, truly seeing its beauty for the first time in years.

From then on, Faela's treasure was no longer her collection of shiny pebbles but the love and joy she spread and received in return. She became a happier, lighter butterfly, finally understanding the wisdom of the ages: "For where your treasure is, there your heart will be also."

"For where your treasure is, there your heart will be also."

The Fable of Baxter: The Dog with Two Homes

IN A QUIET VILLAGE where the river met the rolling hills, there lived Baxter, a jovial dog with a shiny coat and wagging tail. Baxter was unique because he had two homes. One was with Mr. Gold, the wealthiest man in the village who lived in a grand mansion. The other was with Ms. Grace, a humble gardener who had a small but cozy cottage.

Baxter loved the luxury at Mr. Gold's mansion—steak dinners, a plush bed, and all the toys a dog could ever want. But with Ms. Grace, he found something different. She offered him simple meals and a modest bed, but she filled his days with love, play, and long walks in nature.

For a time, Baxter thought he had the best of both worlds. But as the days went by, he realized the burden of serving two masters. Mr. Gold was obsessed with wealth and often left Baxter alone while he went out to make more money. On the other hand, Ms. Grace, although poor in material wealth, was rich in love and companionship.

The villagers often said, "No one can serve two masters, for either he will hate the one and love the other, or he will be devoted to the one and despise the other. You cannot serve God and money."

Feeling the weight of this wisdom, Baxter found himself at a crossroads. One day, Mr. Gold presented him with a diamond-studded collar, a sign of opulence and a symbol of Mr. Gold's priorities. Baxter felt uncomfortable, realizing that the collar represented a life focused solely on material gains.

The very same day, Ms. Grace offered him a simple but meaningful gift—a handmade bandana with the word 'Love' stitched into it. As she tied it around his neck, Baxter felt a warmth spread through him, and he knew where his true home was.

The next morning, Baxter made a choice. He left the grand mansion of Mr. Gold, diamond collar left on the doorstep, and trotted back to the small cottage where Ms. Grace lived. As he approached, Ms. Grace greeted him with a smile and open arms, as if she had been expecting him all along.

For the rest of his days, Baxter lived happily with Ms. Grace, learning the most valuable lesson of his life—that love and true companionship are the only treasures that can bring eternal happiness.

From then on, the villagers often used Baxter's story as a lesson for their children, saying, "Remember, you cannot serve two masters. Make a choice that fills your life with genuine riches—love, friendship, and spiritual contentment."

"No one can serve two masters, for either he will hate the one and love the other, or he will be devoted to the one and despise the other. You cannot serve God and money."

Harmony: The Anxious Hummingbird

IN THE HEART OF RADIANT Rainforest, where the flowers were ever-blooming and the sun perpetually shining, lived Harmony, a petite hummingbird with iridescent feathers. Harmony had one persistent concern that overshadowed her days: she was always anxious about what she would eat, where she would find her next meal, and if her colors were bright enough to fit in.

"My dear Harmony," chirped her wise friend Oliver, the old owl, "why are you always so anxious? Do not be anxious about your life, what you shall eat or what you shall drink, nor about your body, what you shall put on. Is not life more than food, and the body more than clothing?"

But Harmony found it difficult to heed Oliver's wisdom. She flitted about from flower to flower, always worrying about whether she was getting enough nectar, always concerned about her appearance.

One day, a great storm hit Radiant Rainforest. Torrential rain poured, and the wind blew so hard that Harmony couldn't fly. Stricken with worry and unable to gather food, she took refuge under a large mushroom, shivering and frightened.

But then, something magical happened. Despite the storm, Harmony realized she was surrounded by a symphony of life. Ants were sharing their food with one another, a spider was rebuilding its web, and Oliver was giving shelter to smaller birds under his wings.

Once the storm subsided, Harmony noticed that the forest had taken care of itself. The ants still had their food, the spider had spun a beautiful new web, and the birds were singing joyfully as if nothing had happened.

The experience opened her eyes, and she finally understood Oliver's wise words: "Do not be anxious about your life, what you shall eat or what you shall drink, nor about your body, what you shall put on. Is not life more than food, and the body more than clothing?"

From that day on, Harmony chose to live in the present, cherishing each moment and appreciating the beauty around her. She no longer fretted about her next meal or how she looked. Instead, she enjoyed the nectar of each flower as she came to it and took pleasure in the vibrant colors of the world around her.

And so, Harmony found that her life became as radiant as the rainforest itself, teaching all who knew her that the essence of life is to live it fully, without the burden of unnecessary worries.

"Do not be anxious about your life, what you shall eat or what you shall drink, nor about your body, what you shall put on. Is not life more than food, and the body more than clothing?"

The Journey of Tilly: The Squirrel Who Found the Golden Acorn

IN NUTWOOD FOREST, where trees touched the sky and leaves danced to the songs of the wind, lived Tilly, a young squirrel with a restless spirit. Tilly was always in a hurry, scurrying from tree to tree, gathering acorns and stashing them away for the winter. Her life revolved around hoarding acorns, so much so that she missed the beauty of the world around her.

Tilly's neighbor, Grandpa Theo, was a wise old squirrel who had seen many seasons come and go. One day, he said to Tilly, "My dear, you seem to be always worried about acorns. Why don't you take some time to enjoy the beauty around you? Seek first the inner peace, the kingdom of God and his righteousness, and all these things will be added to you."

Tilly was skeptical but intrigued. "A golden acorn?" she thought. "Could such a thing really grant me inner peace?"

With a heart full of curiosity, Tilly embarked on a quest. She traveled through forests and crossed rivers, facing trials and challenges along the way. Yet, despite the hardships, Tilly began to notice something: the journey itself was transforming her.

She started appreciating the rustle of the leaves, the song of the birds, and the serenity of the forest. For the first time, she was living in the moment, experiencing a kind of peace and happiness she had never felt before.

Finally, after what seemed like an eternity, Tilly reached the ancient oak tree. Nestled between its roots was the golden acorn, glowing softly.

As she touched it, a wave of tranquility washed over her, confirming what Grandpa Theo had told her.

Returning to Nutwood Forest, Tilly distributed her excess acorns among her friends and focused on enjoying the present. She still prepared for the winter, but she did it without the anxiety that had once consumed her.

From then on, Tilly lived by Grandpa Theo's wisdom: "But seek first the kingdom of God and his righteousness, and all these things will be added to you." She had everything she needed and more, for she had found the true treasures of life—peace, love, and a sense of purpose.

"But seek first the kingdom of God and his righteousness, and all these things will be added to you."

The Parable of Timmy Turtle: One Step at a Time

IN THE QUIET WATERS of Serene Pond, where lily pads floated like emerald islands and dragonflies hummed lullabies, lived Timmy Turtle. Timmy was a worrier by nature. He constantly fretted about what tomorrow might bring: Will it rain? Will there be enough food? Will the pond freeze over in the winter?

His friend, Freddie Frog, who sunbathed on lily pads and enjoyed each day as it came, often told him, "Do not worry about tomorrow, for tomorrow will worry about itself. Each day has enough trouble of its own."

Despite this advice, Timmy found it hard to relax. That was until the Great Drought hit Serene Pond. The water levels dropped dramatically, and food became scarce. Panic spread among the pond's residents. For the first time, Timmy's worries seemed justified.

But as days passed, Timmy noticed something extraordinary. Despite the scarcity, every day provided just enough for everyone. Freddie Frog would find a few bugs to eat, Mrs. Mallard would catch some small fish for her ducklings, and even Timmy stumbled upon some underwater plants each day. It wasn't plenty, but it was enough.

During the evening gatherings at the pond's edge, the wise elder tortoise, Grandma Tilda, would often say, "Do you see, young ones? We are taken care of each day. Let's not worry about tomorrow and focus on the now. Each day has enough trouble of its own."

As the words sank in, Timmy started to let go of his worries. Instead of fearing the future, he began to live in the present, relishing the food he had for the day, the sun that warmed his shell, and the company of his friends.

Finally, rain clouds gathered, and the Great Drought came to an end. The pond filled up, and life returned to its peaceful routine. But Timmy had changed. He had learned to take life one step, or rather one swim, at a time.

From then on, whenever he felt worry creeping into his thoughts, he'd remember Grandma Tilda's words, "Do not worry about tomorrow, for tomorrow will worry about itself. Each day has enough trouble of its own."

And so, Timmy lived his days more fully, appreciating the simple joys and challenges that each brought, content in the knowledge that life unfolds just as it should—one day at a time.

"Do not worry about tomorrow, for tomorrow will worry about itself. Each day has enough trouble of its own."

The Fable of Fenny Fox: The Forest's Unlikely Hero

IN WHIMSICAL WOODS, a community filled with animals of all shapes and sizes, lived Fenny Fox—a critter with a somewhat troublesome reputation. Many animals had prematurely judged Fenny as mischievous and sly simply because he was a fox. "Do not go near Fenny; he's up to no good," the whispers echoed through the forest.

Wise Walter, an old and thoughtful owl, always advised the creatures, "Do not judge, so that you may not be judged. Each of us is a unique piece in the intricate puzzle of this forest."

But his words mostly fell on deaf ears—until one fateful day.

A ferocious fire broke out at the edge of the forest. Panic spread like wildfire. Bambi the deer, who was known for her grace and poise, stumbled in her haste. She got tangled in some thick vines and couldn't free herself.

Animals rushed past her, saving their own lives. But Fenny Fox stopped, his eyes meeting Bambi's desperate gaze. Ignoring the approaching flames and his own survival instinct, Fenny used his sharp teeth to cut through the vines and free Bambi.

Together, they made it to safety, and the forest community began to see Fenny in a new light. He had risked his life to save another, showing bravery and compassion that belied the judgments cast upon him.

From that moment on, the animals started to realize the truth in Wise Walter's words: "Do not judge, so that you may not be judged."

They began to appreciate each other for who they truly were, and not by the labels they had imposed upon one another.

Fenny Fox became a hero, but more importantly, he became a symbol of the dangers of judging someone before truly knowing them. The community learned a valuable lesson, one that brought them closer and made their forest a more understanding and harmonious place to live.

And so, each animal, from the tiniest insect to the largest bear, lived by the wisdom that had been shared. They stopped judging and started loving, making Whimsical Woods a better place for all its inhabitants.

"Do not judge, so that you may not be judged."

The Fable of Fiona the Frog: Words That Echo

IN THE MYSTICAL POND of Lilypad Landing, Fiona the Frog was known for her insatiable appetite. She would gobble up anything—from flies to small fish, making sure she never missed a meal. The other creatures often judged her for her eating habits, believing her to be careless and impulsive.

"Look at Fiona, always munching on something. She doesn't even think before she eats!" they would say, shaking their heads in disapproval.

However, Fiona was wise in ways that others didn't immediately see. "It is not what goes into the mouth that defiles a person, but what comes out of the mouth; this defiles a person," she would reply, never bothered by the judgment she received.

One day, a dispute broke out among the creatures of Lilypad Landing. Sammy the Snail had lost his shell, and he accused Timmy the Turtle of taking it to replace his own aging shell. Accusations flew, tempers flared, and hurtful words were uttered.

As tensions reached a boiling point, Fiona hopped into the middle of the circle. "Let's pause for a moment and think about what we are saying. Words can hurt more than actions, and once they are out, they can't be taken back."

Chastened, the animals grew silent, realizing the wisdom in Fiona's words. At that moment, Sunny the Squirrel rushed into the clearing, holding Sammy's lost shell. "I found this near the oak tree! Sammy, it must have been carried away by the wind!"

Embarrassed but relieved, Sammy the Snail gratefully took back his shell. Timmy the Turtle was equally relieved and grateful that the truth had come out before his reputation was tarnished further.

After that incident, the animals of Lilypad Landing grew cautious with their words, understanding that their tongues could be sharper than any thorn and more venomous than any bite.

Fiona's appetite for food remained, but what also grew was the creatures' appetite for her wisdom. They learned that while they could consume countless meals, it was the words they emitted that defined who they truly were.

The pond was filled with ripples, not just from the splashing of water but also from the echoes of kind and thoughtful words, proving that what comes out of the mouth indeed defines the spirit of a community.

"It is not what goes into the mouth that defiles a person, but what comes out of the mouth; this defiles a person."

The Story of Oliver the Owl: The Wisdom of Innocence

OLIVER THE OWL WAS the wisest creature in the magical forest of Eldoria. Animals from near and far would travel to seek his advice, admire his extensive library, and listen to his profound insights. Oliver was proud of his wisdom and thought he had all the answers.

One evening, a soft voice echoed through the trees, "Truly, I say to you, unless you turn and become like children, you will never enter the kingdom of heaven."

Startled by the mysterious proclamation, Oliver couldn't sleep. He pondered upon the meaning of these words. "Become like children? But children know so little," he thought to himself.

Days passed, and Oliver's curiosity got the best of him. He decided to observe the children who played in the meadow. They laughed, played games, and their eyes sparkled with wonder and excitement. They seemed so carefree and happy.

Unable to contain his curiosity, Oliver asked them, "Why are you all so happy?"

One of the children, a young rabbit named Rosie, looked up and said, "Because the world is full of fun things to discover!"

"But you have not read the books I have, or studied the ways of the world," Oliver said.

"That may be true," Rosie replied, "but we have joy, friendship, and imagination. We look at the world with wonder and see possibilities, not just facts."

That struck a chord with Oliver. He returned to his library but found himself unable to focus on his tomes and scrolls. Finally, he stepped out of his comfort zone and joined the children in the meadow. At first, he felt foolish, hopping around and playing games. But soon, he felt a joy he had never experienced before.

Days turned into weeks, and something magical happened. The animals who came to seek Oliver's wisdom found him changed, his eyes filled with the same wonder and excitement he had seen in the children. His wisdom was now enriched with a childlike perspective, and the creatures noticed that his advice felt deeper, yet simpler; more profound, yet easy to understand.

Finally, Oliver understood the meaning of the mysterious voice. Wisdom was not just the accumulation of knowledge and experience; it was also the ability to see the world with a child's open heart and boundless imagination.

The animals of Eldoria started visiting not just for advice, but also to join in the games and laughter that Oliver now frequently took part in. Oliver the Owl had found the kingdom of heaven right where he was, hidden in the giggles and joy of youthful hearts.

"Truly, I say to you, unless you turn and become like children, you will never enter the kingdom of heaven."

Grandma Maple: The Garden of Eternal Spring

IN A SMALL VILLAGE where the four seasons took turns ruling the landscape, lived Grandma Maple. She was known far and wide for her magical garden that remained in eternal spring. Roses bloomed, butterflies danced, and the air always carried the scent of fresh lavender. What was even more remarkable was that this enchanting place was always open to the village children.

One day, a committee of elders decided that children should be kept away from the garden. "They are careless and might ruin the flowers," said Elder Oak, a man known for his rigid ways.

When Grandma Maple heard this, her eyes twinkled like morning dew as she said, "Let the little children come to me, and do not hinder them, for the kingdom of heaven belongs to such as these."

Ignoring the decree, Grandma Maple continued to welcome the children into her garden. She even went a step further and began teaching them about each flower, bird, and insect that called her garden home. The children listened intently, their eyes wide with wonder.

News of her defiance reached the council of elders, and they arrived to confront her. "Why do you disobey our decree? Do you not think we have wisdom in our years?"

With a kind smile, Grandma Maple guided them through her garden. To their surprise, the garden was more beautiful than ever. The flowers shone more vividly, and the air was even sweeter. As they reached the center of the garden, they saw a breathtaking sight: a new tree had sprung up, its branches laden with fruits of all kinds.

"This tree is called the Tree of Eternal Spring," said Grandma Maple, "and it has grown because the children planted seeds of joy, wonder, and love in this garden."

Confused, Elder Oak asked, "But how is that possible? We thought they would ruin your beautiful garden!"

Grandma Maple replied, "Sometimes, wisdom and age make us forget the simple yet profound truths that children understand. Their purity, innocence, and wonder are like nourishment to the soul of this garden. They remind us that the most important things in life aren't rules and regulations but joy, love, and wonder."

The elders felt a warmth spread through their hearts. It was as if the years had been peeled away and they were standing in the garden as children once more. From that day on, they revoked their decree and even began visiting the garden themselves, often joining the children in discovering the little miracles that bloomed each day.

As for Grandma Maple, her garden continued to bloom in eternal spring, a slice of heaven where age didn't matter and where the kingdom belonged to hearts that remained forever young.

"Let the little children come to me, and do not hinder them, for the kingdom of heaven belongs to such as these."

The Parable of Carson the Camel: The Eye of the Needle

IN THE BUSTLING DESERT city of Mirage, where traders from all lands came to buy and sell, lived Carson the Camel. Carson was unlike any other camel—he was owned by the richest merchant in the city, Gilbert Goldspur.

Carson carried the heaviest loads of gold, spices, and precious stones. He wore a saddle adorned with shimmering jewels and plush, colorful fabric. People often said, "Carson is the richest camel in all the lands!"

However, Carson was always intrigued by the simple lives of the camels in the nomadic caravans that passed by. He saw them carrying families, singing around campfires, and exploring new lands. They had no riches, yet they seemed so full of joy and contentment.

One evening, Carson heard an old woman utter a strange saying: "It is easier for a camel to go through the eye of a needle than for a rich man to enter the kingdom of God."

Confused and intrigued, Carson decided to find out what this meant. He approached Nora the Nomad, a wise camel who had traveled through deserts and across mountains.

"Why is it easier for a camel to go through the eye of a needle than for a rich man to enter the kingdom of God?" Carson asked.

Nora chuckled and replied, "Ah, it's a metaphor, young one. The eye of a needle is small, almost impossible for anything big to pass through. Likewise, when someone's life is burdened by the pursuit of riches, it becomes almost impossible for them to find true happiness—the kind that feels like heaven."

Carson was thoughtful. "So, you're saying the kingdom of God isn't a place but a state of happiness and contentment?"

"Exactly," Nora nodded.

Determined to experience this for himself, Carson shed his extravagant saddle, jewels, and other adornments. He felt lighter and, for the first time, unburdened.

Gilbert Goldspur was furious at first, but seeing Carson so happy and full of life made him ponder. Slowly, even he started letting go of his endless pursuit of wealth, focusing instead on the simple joys that life had to offer.

Carson began accompanying the nomadic caravans, exploring the world and carrying families and their dreams instead of just material riches. He found that the joy he experienced in these simple acts was more fulfilling than any luxury he had known before.

In time, Carson became a legend, not for his riches but for his wisdom and contentment. He had successfully passed through the proverbial 'eye of the needle,' finding a kingdom not of material wealth, but one rich in joy, love, and peace—a kingdom that truly felt like heaven.

"It is easier for a camel to go through the eye of a needle than for a rich man to enter the kingdom of God."

The Story of Sparrow and the Impossible Seed: A Lesson in Faith

ONCE UPON A TIME, IN a peaceful valley surrounded by towering mountains, lived a humble sparrow named Sammy. Sammy loved singing, and his cheerful melodies would greet the dawn and welcome the dusk. However, he harbored a secret wish—to see a garden of magical Sun-Star flowers bloom in the barren land next to his nest.

The Sun-Star flowers were no ordinary flowers. They were golden and emitted a heavenly fragrance. They were said to bloom only once every hundred years and required a special type of seed that was extremely rare.

One day, an ancient turtle named Tilly came to the valley carrying a mysterious seed on her back. "This," she said, "is the last known Sun-Star seed. They say it's impossible for it to bloom now, but I believe you have the power to make it happen."

"Why me?" Sammy asked, his feathers quivering in excitement and disbelief.

"Because with God, all things are possible. You just need to have faith," Tilly replied before leaving, her job done.

Eager but nervous, Sammy took the seed and planted it in the barren ground. Days turned into weeks, weeks into months, but the seed showed no sign of life. Doubts filled Sammy's heart, but he remembered Tilly's words: "With God, all things are possible."

Determined, Sammy continued to sing to the seed every morning and evening, watering it with morning dew and keeping faith that it would bloom. Then, something miraculous happened. One day, as the sun began to rise, the ground trembled ever so slightly, and a tiny sprout pushed its way through the soil.

Sammy couldn't believe his eyes! His heart was filled with an indescribable joy as the sprout grew taller each day, finally bursting into a magnificent Sun-Star flower. Its golden petals shimmered in the sunlight, and its heavenly fragrance filled the valley.

Word of the impossible feat spread like wildfire, and creatures from all corners of the land came to witness the miracle. They were astounded and wanted to know Sammy's secret.

With a humble chirp, Sammy said, "I did not perform this miracle; I simply believed that it was possible. When you have faith, truly, all things are possible."

From then on, the valley was no longer just a place of natural beauty; it became a landmark of faith and possibility. Sammy continued to sing, not just for himself but for all those who needed a reminder that miracles happen when you believe they can.

And so, in a valley that once was barren, faith had planted a garden, proving once again that with God, all things are possible.

"With God, all things are possible."

Harmony Hedgehog: A Journey to Wholehearted Love

IN THE CHARMING VILLAGE of Woodland Hollow, where the leaves danced in the wind and the rivers hummed their eternal songs, lived Harmony the Hedgehog. She was named for her quest to live a life of balance, continually seeking to love God with all her heart, soul, and mind.

Harmony was friends with everyone—from Bentley the Bear to Wendy the Weasel. She loved reading, exploring, and helping others. Her days were filled with both excitement and peaceful solitude, but Harmony always felt something was missing.

A wise old owl named Oliver lived atop a grand oak tree. Harmony went to him, asking how she could achieve her quest to wholly love God.

"Ah," Oliver said, eyes sparkling, "loving God with all your heart, soul, and mind is a life's journey. It's not just about feeling but about intentional living."

"How can I begin?" Harmony asked.

Oliver instructed her to embark on three quests—one for her heart, one for her soul, and one for her mind.

The Quest of the Heart: For her heart's quest, Harmony helped build homes for the homeless critters. While working alongside Bentley, she poured her heart into every nail and plank. As the last home was completed, she felt an overwhelming sense of love. "This," she realized, "is loving God with all my heart—by serving others."

The Quest of the Soul: Next was her soul's quest. She retreated into the Whispering Woods for a time of solitude and meditation. As Harmony sat in silence, listening to the wind rustle through the trees and the rivers whisper, her soul felt deeply connected to God. She understood that her soul could express love for God through stillness and connection with the world around her.

The Quest of the Mind: For her mind's quest, Harmony visited the Library of Leaves, where she poured over ancient texts and philosophies about God. With Wendy the Weasel, who loved intellectual discussions, she engaged in deep conversations. Through this, Harmony realized that she could love God with her mind by continually seeking wisdom and understanding.

Having completed her quests, Harmony returned to Oliver.

"Feel any different?" he asked.

"I feel complete," Harmony said, "I feel like I'm finally on the path to loving God wholly—heart, soul, and mind."

Oliver nodded approvingly, "You've made a good start, Harmony. Remember, the journey is ongoing. Keep loving, seeking, and serving."

And so, Harmony became a living example of wholehearted devotion. Her heart was filled with love for others, her soul found peace in God's presence, and her mind continually sought to understand the world's divine intricacies.

In this way, Harmony Hedgehog came to know the richness of loving God with all her heart, all her soul, and all her mind—a quest that filled her life with untold beauty and balance.

"You shall love the Lord your God with all your heart, and with all your soul, and with all your mind."

Benny the Badger and the Golden Rule

IN THE QUAINT, BUSTLING animal village of Meadowgrove, lived Benny the Badger. Benny was a fine builder, always busy with constructing homes, mending fences, and fixing roofs. But despite his good work, Benny was a bit gruff and usually kept to himself.

The other animals often wondered, "Why is Benny so distant? He's an excellent builder but seems so aloof."

One fine day, the Council of Elders announced a village festival to celebrate the harvest. Each animal was invited to contribute to the festivities. Benny, naturally, was assigned the task of setting up the stage.

During the preparations, Benny noticed that a family of squirrels, new to Meadowgrove, had no place to stay. They looked lost and forlorn. Benny's first instinct was to mind his own business, but then he remembered an ancient teaching: "You shall love your neighbor as yourself."

Benny pondered the words, thinking about his comfortable burrow, the warmth it offered during cold nights, and the safety it provided. He thought, "What if I were in their place, with no home and new to the village?"

Putting aside his aloofness, Benny approached the squirrel family. "Hi, I'm Benny the Badger. I noticed you don't have a place to stay. Would you like some help building a home?"

The squirrel family looked up, their eyes shining with gratitude. "Oh, thank you! We would be so grateful for your help," said the mother squirrel, her voice tinged with relief.

Benny immediately set to work, and with his skilled paws, built a cozy treehouse for the family. When he finished, the young squirrel kids ran up to him and hugged him tightly, their tiny hearts filled with joy.

On the day of the harvest festival, the atmosphere was jubilant, and the stage stood strong and beautiful. When Benny walked onto the stage to receive a Community Spirit Award, the applause was thunderous. Benny felt something he had not felt in years—a sense of belonging and warmth.

After that day, Benny continued to be a builder, but he built much more than just structures. He built friendships and a sense of community. He learned the true meaning of the words, "You shall love your neighbor as yourself," and became not just a builder, but also a beloved neighbor.

And so, the animals of Meadowgrove learned a valuable lesson—that loving your neighbor is not merely an act of kindness but a foundation on which a loving community can be built.

"You shall love your neighbor as yourself."

Timmy Turtle: A Change of Heart

ONCE UPON A TIME IN the enchanting world of Forest Glen, lived Timmy the Turtle. Timmy was well-known for being a mischief-maker, always involved in one prank or another. Although he was a bundle of fun, his actions often led to trouble for others.

In the center of Forest Glen stood the Ancient Tree, known as the heart of the forest and the keeper of wisdom. The Ancient Tree, it was said, knew secrets about the Kingdom of God, a realm of pure love, compassion, and righteousness.

One morning, a proclamation was heard echoing through the forest:

"The time is fulfilled, and the Kingdom of God is at hand; repent and believe in the gospel."

Timmy was puzzled. "Repent and believe? What could that mean?"

Being naturally curious, he decided to seek guidance from the wise Ancient Tree.

"My child," said the Ancient Tree when Timmy asked for advice, "the Kingdom of God is not just a place; it's a way of living—filled with love, understanding, and virtue. To be part of it, you must change your ways. You must repent for your mischief and believe in the gospel of kindness and love."

Timmy took the Ancient Tree's words to heart. He decided it was time for a change. Instead of pranking others, he began to help them. He aided Barry the Beaver in constructing his dam, and he assisted Fiona the Firefly in lighting up the night for a forest gathering.

Soon, the animals of Forest Glen started noticing the change in Timmy. Where once they would brace themselves for his pranks, now they looked forward to his helpful presence.

Days turned into weeks, and Timmy's old ways became a distant memory. Feeling happier and more fulfilled, he returned to the Ancient Tree.

"You have done well," said the Ancient Tree, leaves shimmering in the golden sunlight. "You have understood that the Kingdom of God is a realm of love, and by changing your ways, you have become part of it."

From then on, Timmy the Turtle became a legend in Forest Glen—not as a mischief-maker, but as a wise and kind turtle who knew the true meaning of repentance and belief in goodness.

And as for the Kingdom of God, it was not just a tale told by the Ancient Tree, but a living reality seen in the love, kindness, and harmony that filled Forest Glen.

"The time is fulfilled, and the kingdom of God is at hand; repent and believe in the gospel."

Carly Caterpillar: The Journey to Transformation

IN A SECLUDED MEADOW filled with colorful flowers and buzzing bees, lived Carly the Caterpillar. She led a simple life, munching on leaves and enjoying the comfort of her home under the shade of a large mushroom. Life was good, but Carly couldn't shake off a feeling of incompleteness.

A message, almost like a whisper from the wind, reached her one day: "Take up your cross and follow me."

Carly was puzzled but intrigued. "Take up my cross? What could that possibly mean?"

Determined to find answers, she set off on a journey toward the Wise Oak, a tree known for its profound wisdom. The journey was not easy. She had to crawl through brambles, navigate rocky terrains, and evade predatory birds. But these challenges, her crosses, shaped her in ways she never imagined. She learned patience, courage, and the art of perseverance.

Finally reaching the Wise Oak, Carly asked, "I've heard a message saying 'Take up your cross and follow me.' What does it mean?"

The Wise Oak rustled its leaves thoughtfully and said, "Taking up your cross means embracing the challenges and sacrifices required for growth and transformation. It's an invitation to journey toward a better version of yourself, even if that path is laden with difficulties."

Enlightened and inspired, Carly thanked the Wise Oak and made her way back home. She thought deeply about what she had learned and understood that her 'cross' was the challenge of transformation that lay ahead—the process of becoming a butterfly.

With newfound resolve, Carly began the arduous process of creating a cocoon, her personal cross that required sacrifice, solitude, and patience. After what seemed like an eternity, she emerged as a beautiful butterfly, her wings shimmering in the radiant sunlight.

Carly returned to her meadow not just as another creature, but as a symbol of hope and transformation. The other insects looked at her in awe, amazed at her metamorphosis.

"Wow! How did you do it?" they would ask.

With a smile, Carly would often say, "By taking up my cross and following a path that led to my true self. And you can do it, too. We all can."

And so, the meadow became a place of not just beauty but inspiration, as more creatures began to take up their crosses—whatever they might be—in their own journeys towards transformation.

"Take up your cross and follow me."

Benny the Brave Bunny: The Paradox of the Lost and Found

IN A FOREST KNOWN AS Mystic Grove, a rabbit named Benny the Brave Bunny was renowned for his daring escapades. He was always eager to explore, to find new treasures, and to be the star of the forest. But despite his name and brave reputation, Benny still felt an unexplainable emptiness inside him.

One day, an echoing message drifted through the forest, stirring the hearts of all its inhabitants: "For whoever would save his life will lose it, but whoever loses his life for my sake and the gospel's will save it."

The message puzzled Benny. "Save my life by losing it? How could that possibly make sense?"

Intrigued, Benny decided to seek advice from Sage the Wise Owl, a creature so ancient, it was said that he'd known the forest when it was still a single sapling.

Upon hearing Benny's query, Sage looked deep into his eyes and spoke, "Ah, the paradox of life. To truly understand it, you must experience it, Benny. It's not about seeking glory or personal gain, but about giving yourself for the greater good."

Benny nodded but wasn't entirely sure what to make of Sage's words. Soon enough, though, he got the opportunity to put them to the test.

A wildfire broke out in Mystic Grove. All the animals were terrified and scampered about, seeking refuge. Benny realized he knew a way to divert a nearby stream to extinguish the fire but doing so would destroy the treasure he had been collecting for years, hidden in a burrow near the stream.

Remembering the paradoxical wisdom he'd heard, Benny made a choice. He led the animals in a team effort to divert the stream, sacrificing his prized possessions to save the forest.

As the water flowed and quenched the fire, something miraculous happened. Benny felt a joy he had never felt before. The emptiness inside him was replaced by a sense of fulfillment and peace.

The other animals hailed him as a hero, but Benny realized that his true heroism didn't lie in saving the day. It lay in understanding the profound truth that by losing what he thought he needed to save—his treasure—he had gained something far more valuable: a sense of purpose and the deep joy of altruism.

From then on, Benny lived not just as a brave bunny, but as a wise and humble one, teaching all who would listen about the paradox of the lost and found, and how sometimes the path to true fulfillment lies in giving, not taking.

"For whoever would save his life will lose it, but whoever loses his life for my sake and the gospel's will save it."

Fergus the Fox: The Price of the Golden Acorn

ONCE UPON A TIME, IN the mystical Whispering Woods, lived Fergus the Fox—a clever and ambitious creature who dreamed of unparalleled riches and comfort. A rumor circulated around the forest about a legendary Golden Acorn that granted immense power and wealth to whoever possessed it. Naturally, Fergus was consumed by the idea of finding this treasure.

The woods whispered again, this time with a cautionary message: "For what does it profit a man to gain the whole world and forfeit his soul?"

Fergus heard the saying but dismissed it, thinking, "What nonsense! How could gaining the world be a loss?"

Ignoring the wise words of the forest, Fergus set out on an expedition. He outsmarted wolves, crossed treacherous rivers, and scaled towering trees, all in search of the mythical Golden Acorn.

Finally, he found it, resting atop a pedestal in a hidden cavern. As soon as he laid his paws on the Golden Acorn, he felt a surge of power, and a mountain of gold and jewels rose from the ground around him. Fergus was ecstatic; he had gained what he thought was the world.

Soon, Fergus built a lavish den, filled with jewels and fine furniture. But to protect his treasures, he became increasingly suspicious and isolated. He even pushed away his family and friends, thinking they might take his wealth away from him. The once cheerful and social fox became a recluse, drowning in his own fortune.

One fateful night, a storm swept through Whispering Woods. Lightning struck and fires spread, threatening the entire forest. The community of animals united to fight the flames, but Fergus was too busy safeguarding his materialistic world to lend a paw.

Despite the community's best efforts, the fire reached Fergus's den. His possessions melted and his once-adored golden acorn was reduced to molten metal. Fergus, now realizing the gravity of his choices, felt emptier than ever.

Remembering the forgotten message of the woods, Fergus finally understood its truth: he had gained worldly possessions but had lost his soul, his community, and his happiness in the process.

With humility, Fergus rejoined his community, helping them rebuild what was lost in the fire. And as he let go of his greed and reconnected with his loved ones, he felt richer than he ever felt with his treasures.

From that day on, Fergus became a guardian of the Whispering Woods, sharing the cautionary tale of the Golden Acorn and the irreplaceable value of community, love, and the soul.

"For what does it profit a man to gain the whole world and forfeit his soul?"

Tessa the Turtle: The Heart That Forgave

IN THE SERENE WATERS of Sapphire Lake lived Tessa the Turtle, a kind-hearted creature known for her wisdom and compassion. Life was tranquil, save for the occasional disruptions from Perry the Pike, a fish with a rather contentious personality. Perry liked to taunt and hassle the inhabitants of Sapphire Lake just for the sheer fun of it.

The lake's timeless wisdom whispered to its residents: "Love your enemies, and pray for those who persecute you."

Many animals found this advice challenging, especially when it came to Perry. But Tessa took the wisdom to heart and made a decision to be different.

One sunny afternoon, Perry got caught in a tangle of water weeds while he was darting around. The more he struggled, the tighter the weeds constricted him. Seeing his distress, most of the lake's residents chose to ignore him, thinking, "It serves him right."

Tessa, however, felt a different calling. Remembering the lake's wisdom, she swam up to Perry and gently began to free him from the water weeds. Perry was stunned by her kindness.

"Why are you helping me? Haven't I been awful to you?" he gasped, still somewhat tangled.

Tessa smiled, "That may be true, but the lake teaches us to love even those who are difficult to love. And so, I pray for your well-being, Perry."

Finally freed, Perry felt a warmth he hadn't felt before—a mix of embarrassment, relief, and a budding sense of gratitude. From that moment, something shifted in him. While he didn't transform overnight, Perry began to question his previous actions and, over time, started to change his ways.

As for Tessa, her act of kindness echoed throughout Sapphire Lake, encouraging others to look past their grudges and grievances. The wisdom that she had embraced became a newfound philosophy for the whole community.

Years later, an elder Perry often shared the story of his entanglement and liberation, emphasizing the transformative power of love and prayer, even for those who once caused suffering.

And so, the residents of Sapphire Lake lived with greater harmony and understanding, all thanks to Tessa's forgiving heart that had put timeless wisdom into action.

"Love your enemies, and pray for those who persecute you."

Benny the Bear: The Golden Pawprint

IN THE COZY FOREST of Harmony Hills lived Benny the Bear, a jovial and social animal who loved nothing more than sharing honey and berries with his friends. The forest was a tapestry of friendships, although there was always room for improvement. One day, an ancient oak tree in the heart of the forest shared its wisdom with the inhabitants: "Do unto others as you would have them do unto you."

Benny, who always believed in sharing and kindness, thought this was an excellent guideline for life. To spread this message, he decided to organize a "Golden Pawprint Day," where each animal would perform a good deed for another.

When the day arrived, Benny went out of his way to help others. He shared his honey with Wendy the Woodpecker, helped Danny the Deer find his lost acorns, and even sang a lullaby to help Lilly the Lark's babies sleep. Benny's actions were not only generous but also intentional—he was treating others the way he would like to be treated.

News of "Golden Pawprint Day" spread like wildfire, inspiring others. Wendy the Woodpecker drilled tiny holes in hard-to-reach places for Squirrel families to store food. Danny the Deer helped clear leaves from the burrow entrance of Tommy the Tortoise. And Lilly the Lark flew up to the tallest tree to keep watch for dangers, giving Marcy the Mouse a break from her usual patrol.

By sunset, Benny felt a sense of fulfillment unlike anything else. And just when he thought the day was over, he returned to his den to find it filled with all sorts of goodies—fresh berries from Barbara the

Bunny, a new cozy rug woven by Sally the Spider, and even a thank-you note scribed by Oliver the Owl, who was known for his wisdom.

The community of Harmony Hills discovered something extraordinary that day: the magic of treating others as you would like to be treated. This simple rule created a ripple effect, transforming their everyday interactions and making their bonds stronger than ever.

And so, each year, "Golden Pawprint Day" became a cherished tradition, a day to honor and spread the ancient wisdom of the oak tree, reminding everyone that in the path of kindness, the giver is often as blessed as the receiver.

"Do unto others as you would have them do unto you."

Fiona the Fox: The Journey to the Whispering Oak

IN THE MAGICAL FOREST of Enchanted Echoes, a legendary oak tree stood tall. It was called the Whispering Oak, said to have the wisdom of the ages. It was rumored that anyone who approached the tree with a sincere question would receive an answer. The saying amongst the forest dwellers was, "Ask, and it will be given to you; seek, and you will find; knock, and it will be opened to you."

Fiona the Fox was a young and curious animal, always asking questions and eager to learn. One day, she decided she wanted to know how to bring lasting happiness to her woodland friends. So, she embarked on a journey to find the Whispering Oak.

The path was filled with challenges. Thick thorns, confusing mazes, and deep rivers were just a few of the obstacles she encountered. Yet, with every difficulty, Fiona remembered the forest saying and asked herself, "What can I learn here? How can this guide me?" In doing so, she found innovative ways to overcome each challenge.

Finally, after what seemed like an eternity, Fiona reached the Whispering Oak. With bated breath, she asked, "How can I bring lasting happiness to my friends?"

A soft voice from the tree responded, "True happiness comes from understanding and love. Listen to your friends, understand their needs, and offer your love and support."

With newfound wisdom, Fiona thanked the Whispering Oak and returned home. Her journey had made her realize the value of asking for guidance, seeking wisdom, and knocking on doors of opportunity. In following this advice, she found the answer she was looking for.

Back in her community, Fiona began practicing what the Whispering Oak had taught her. She listened carefully to her friends, offering them a shoulder to lean on, helping them in their tasks, and encouraging them to share their worries and joys. Slowly but surely, her friends started to feel happier, more understood, and loved.

Word spread quickly through Enchanted Echoes that Fiona had become a source of happiness and wisdom for all. Many animals now wanted to go on their journey to the Whispering Oak, and Fiona told them the saying that guided her, reminding them that the answers they seek are often closer than they think.

"Ask, and it will be given to you; seek, and you will find; knock, and it will be opened to you."

Leo the Lion: The Gift of Eternal Love

ONCE UPON A TIME, IN the serene savanna of Harmony Hills, lived Leo the Lion—mighty, gentle, and wise. He was a loving father to his son, Luca, who was young, curious, and full of life. The animals of Harmony Hills looked up to Leo not just as their leader but also as a beacon of wisdom and compassion.

The savanna was often threatened by dark clouds of doom, manifesting as natural disasters, famine, or disease. Each time, Leo stood his ground, defending the territory and ensuring the welfare of his subjects. However, he knew that the cycle of doom would continue to haunt the savanna unless a sacrifice was made to bring eternal peace.

One day, a shooting star lit up the night sky, and Leo took it as a sign. The oracle elephant, Ella, told him, "For God so loved the world, that he gave his only begotten Son, that whoever believes in him should not perish, but have eternal life."

Tears in his eyes, Leo explained to Luca that he needed to embark on a journey to the Sacred Grove—a mystical land beyond the Seven Rivers—to obtain the Elixir of Light that would permanently scatter the dark clouds of doom.

Understanding the magnitude of the mission, Luca bravely said, "I will go, Father. If my journey can bring everlasting peace to our home, then I will gladly accept this quest."

Filled with pride, yet torn inside, Leo watched as Luca crossed the Seven Rivers and disappeared into the horizon. Months passed with no word from him, and the savanna held its collective breath.

Then, one fateful day, Luca returned, holding a glowing vial of the Elixir of Light. The animals cheered and wept as Luca poured the elixir into the Heart Spring—the central water source of Harmony Hills.

As soon as the liquid touched the water, a ripple of light burst forth, reaching every corner of the savanna. The dark clouds of doom were instantly dispelled, replaced by a radiant, everlasting sunshine. The land blossomed as never before; it was as if every living being had been granted eternal life through love and belief in the courageous act of Luca.

From that day forth, the animals of Harmony Hills lived in everlasting peace, never forgetting the sacrifice and love that brought them their salvation. They realized that the path to eternal life was not through evading hardships but through faith, love, and the courage to make sacrifices for the greater good.

And so, Leo and Luca sat atop Pride Rock, basking in the eternal sunshine, their hearts full of a love that was as endless as life itself.

"For God so loved the world, that he gave his only begotten Son, that whoever believes in him should not perish, but have eternal life."

Rosa the Rabbit: The Meadow of Abundance

IN A SECLUDED WOODLAND, teeming with critters and flora, lived Rosa the Rabbit—a creature unlike any other. While most rabbits were content in their burrows, Rosa yearned for more. She'd heard of an old saying: "I came that they may have life and have it abundantly."

Rosa was intrigued. What did it mean to live life abundantly? It wasn't just about having more carrots to eat or a bigger burrow to live in. It was a puzzle she felt compelled to solve for the sake of her woodland friends.

After weeks of pondering, Rosa had an idea. With her tiny paws, she began to dig a new kind of burrow. Instead of just digging downwards, she dug upwards and outwards, creating a labyrinth that connected different parts of the forest. This allowed the animals to travel more easily and made the community more connected than ever before.

But Rosa didn't stop there. With the help of the industrious beavers, she created a water canal that brought water to dry areas of the forest. Now, fields that were once barren began to bloom.

And still, Rosa felt there was more to do. She visited the wise old owl, Oliver, who was known for his extensive knowledge. "How can I help our friends live life more abundantly?" Rosa asked.

"The key is not just in resources, but in experiences and relationships," Oliver said. "Why not organize events where everyone can learn something new or create stronger bonds?"

Inspired by this new insight, Rosa started what became a monthly tradition in the forest—The Day of Sharing. On this day, every animal taught something they were good at. The squirrels taught how to store food efficiently, the birds gave singing lessons, and the foxes showed how to navigate through the woods swiftly.

As time passed, not only did the woodland thrive, but the animals also became well-rounded, happier, and more connected. They thanked Rosa for her wisdom and her unending quest for abundance. Rosa smiled, for she now understood what it meant to live life abundantly—it was to grow, to share, and to love unconditionally.

And so, every creature in the woodland found their own sense of abundance, whether it was in the bloom of a new flower, the laughter of a neighbor, or the simple joy of being alive.

"I came that they may have life and have it abundantly."

Una the Unicorn: The Symphony of Unity

IN A MAGICAL FOREST lived Una the Unicorn, a creature of mystical powers, known for her radiant horn that could heal and her eyes that sparkled like constellations. Una had a twin brother, Orion, who was equally magical but in different ways. His hooves could bring forth springs of fresh water, and his mane was as radiant as the dawn.

Though the forest was home to many magical beings, none were as revered as Una and Orion. Still, the forest was divided, with some creatures drawn more to Una's healing abilities, while others admired Orion for his life-giving powers.

Rumors spread, creating discord among the creatures. Some said, "Una's healing is the essence of magic!" Others countered, "No, it's Orion's power of creation that keeps the forest alive!"

Tension reached a peak, with the forest threatened to be torn apart. Una and Orion felt the weight of the discord deeply, for they loved all creatures and each other immensely.

It was then that Una announced, "I and Orion are one. Our magic comes from the same source, the unity that binds us."

To prove it, they stood together at the heart of the forest, hooves touching and horns gleaming in the moonlight. As they whispered ancient spells, a marvel occurred. Una's horn and Orion's mane radiated an intense light, merging into a single dazzling ray.

This beautiful light beam shot up into the sky and then rained down like a shower of stars, healing broken wings and filling dry ponds.

Flowers bloomed instantly, and laughter filled the air. The creatures felt an overwhelming sense of peace and unity.

Moved to tears, they realized their folly. There was no separation; the magic of Una and Orion, just like their love, was inseparable. It was a powerful manifestation of unity and oneness, transcending any division.

From that day on, the creatures of the forest lived in harmony, knowing that the true magic was in unity, and in the love that bound them all together. They celebrated Una and Orion, not as two separate beings, but as a single miracle that enriched their lives.

So remember, dear ones, in every walk of life, the power of unity is the greatest magic of all.

"I and the Father are one."

Sora the Sparrow: A Feather of Obedience

IN THE WARM EMBRACE of a sleepy valley lived Sora the Sparrow. Though small and often overlooked, Sora was devoted to Willow the Wise, a majestic old tree at the center of the valley. Willow the Wise was revered for its ancient wisdom and the shelter it provided to countless animals.

Willow had one simple commandment for all animals: "Protect the small pond beside me, for it is the source of life in the valley."

Sora loved Willow deeply, believing in the tree's wisdom and its vision for a balanced ecosystem. To show her love, Sora took the commandment to heart. Every morning, she would visit the pond, making sure no animal polluted it or took more water than needed.

Many animals admired Sora's devotion but thought it was unnecessary. "Why not enjoy the abundance without worrying about rules?" said Larry the Lizard.

Sora would kindly reply, "If you love Willow as I do, you will understand that keeping its commandment is not a burden but a joy."

Time passed, and a severe drought befell the land. Rivers dried up, and trees withered. Yet, the pond beside Willow remained fresh and clear. Animals from nearby lands came to the valley, seeking relief. Thanks to the preserved pond, Willow could offer them sanctuary.

The valley dwellers finally understood the wisdom of Willow's commandment and Sora's devoted compliance. Larry the Lizard humbly said, "Your love for Willow not only saved the pond but all of us. You've shown us that true love manifests in action, in keeping the commandments of the one you love."

From then on, all animals took turns guarding the pond, each reflecting on Sora's wisdom. They realized that in their acts of obedience, they found the highest form of love—a love that preserves and nurtures life.

So children, when you love someone or something deeply, you honor their wishes naturally. For love is not just in words but in the actions that uphold the values of the beloved.

"If you love me, you will keep my commandments."

Little Thistle and the Hidden Meadow

ONCE UPON A TIME IN a dense, magical forest, lived a tiny hedgehog named Little Thistle.

Little Thistle was a curious creature, always poking around and asking questions. He was kind and friendly but sometimes forgot to clean up his mess or say "please" and "thank you." Little Thistle loved exploring the forest, but he'd heard tales of a mysterious, hidden meadow that was said to be a slice of heaven on earth.

The older animals often whispered, "Change your ways, young one, for the Hidden Meadow is near." But Little Thistle didn't really understand what they meant.

One bright morning, Little Thistle decided he would search for this hidden meadow.

He scampered over hills, waded through streams, and pushed through thick bushes. Finally, he found himself at the entrance of a dark tunnel. A wise old owl named Oliver was perched on a branch near the tunnel's entrance.

"Where do you think you're going, Little Thistle?" Oliver asked, narrowing his eyes.

"I'm trying to find the Hidden Meadow," said Little Thistle, "I heard it's like heaven on earth!"

Oliver chuckled, "Ah yes, it's a place of immense beauty and peace. But remember, 'Repent, for the kingdom of heaven is near.'"

Confused, Little Thistle asked, "What does 'repent' mean, Oliver?"

"Ah, to repent means to acknowledge one's mistakes and strive to be better," explained Oliver. "The Hidden Meadow only reveals itself to those who are kind-hearted and well-mannered."

Little Thistle pondered for a moment. He remembered how he'd been careless in the past, leaving trash around and not being polite.

"Thank you, Oliver, I understand now. I must go and make amends," said Little Thistle.

With newfound determination, Little Thistle set off back into the forest.

He picked up all the trash he had left behind, apologized to the animals he had been rude to, and promised himself to be more considerate in the future.

Feeling lighter and happier, Little Thistle returned to the tunnel entrance where Oliver was still perched.

"I have repented, Oliver. Will the Hidden Meadow welcome me now?" Little Thistle asked.

Oliver smiled warmly, "Let's find out."

This time, when Little Thistle entered the tunnel, he felt a magical warmth surrounding him. When he emerged on the other side, he couldn't believe his eyes! There it was, the Hidden Meadow, glowing with an ethereal light, filled with flowers of unimaginable colors and butterflies that sparkled like jewels.

"You have found the Hidden Meadow, Little Thistle, for you have learned the true meaning of repentance," said Oliver who had followed him.

From that day on, Little Thistle became the kindest and most polite hedgehog in the forest, often visiting the Hidden Meadow, which remained a slice of heaven on earth for him.

And so, the tale of Little Thistle reminds us all that heaven is not a place you find; it's a state of heart and mind.

"Repent, for the kingdom of heaven is near."

Harvest Mouse and the Bread of Wisdom

IN THE COZY CORNER of Windy Willow Woods, lived a small harvest mouse named Hazel.

Hazel loved bread more than anything in the world. She believed that bread was the answer to all of life's problems. Had a bad day? Bread. Feeling sad? Bread. Need to celebrate? Bread!

However, no matter how much bread Hazel ate, she felt something was missing. The wise old tortoise, named Timothy, noticed Hazel's discontent.

"Ah, my young friend, you seem troubled," said Timothy.

"I don't understand, Timothy. I have all the bread in the world, but I still feel empty inside," replied Hazel.

Timothy looked at Hazel and quoted an ancient saying: "Man does not live on bread alone, but on every word that comes from the mouth of God."

Hazel tilted her head in confusion. "What does that mean, Timothy?"

"It means, dear Hazel, that while bread may feed your body, there are other things like wisdom, love, and kindness that feed your soul. Have you ever tried seeking those?"

Intrigued and slightly skeptical, Hazel decided to give it a try.

Over the next few days, Hazel went on a journey throughout Windy Willow Woods. She listened to the songs of the birds, which taught her about joy. She observed the teamwork of ants, learning about unity. She even watched the river flow and learned about the virtue of patience.

However, it was the words of Timothy that fed her soul the most. Every evening, Hazel would sit by Timothy's rock, and he would share ancient wisdom, tales of virtue, and lessons on kindness.

Hazel felt like a new mouse. She still loved bread, but it was no longer the center of her life. She felt nourished in a way that bread alone had never managed to achieve.

One day, a terrible storm hit Windy Willow Woods.

Trees were falling, rivers were overflowing, and many animals were in distress. Hazel, filled with the wisdom and virtues she had learned, was instrumental in guiding her friends to safety. She used her newfound patience to calm the panicked, her understanding of unity to organize a rescue, and her joy to uplift those who were scared.

After the storm had passed, everyone gathered around Timothy's rock.

"You've shown immense bravery and wisdom, Hazel," Timothy declared. "You've proven that indeed, 'Man does not live on bread alone, but on every word that comes from the mouth of God.'"

Hazel felt her heart swell with happiness. She finally understood what Timothy meant. Bread might fill the stomach, but wisdom, love, and kindness filled the soul.

From that day on, Hazel didn't just feast on bread; she feasted on the words of wisdom, the acts of kindness, and the love she shared with everyone in Windy Willow Woods.

And so, she was never hungry again—not in the way she used to be.

"Man does not live on bread alone, but on every word that comes from the mouth of God."

Lumi the Firefly and the Night of Wonders

DEEP IN THE HEART OF Whispering Woods, where trees were tall and the night sky full of stars, lived Lumi the Firefly.

Lumi was not like other fireflies; her glow was brighter, warmer, and more enchanting. Yet, Lumi was shy and often hid her light under a leaf, worried that others might find it too dazzling or overwhelming.

Elder Willow, the wise tree at the center of the woods, noticed Lumi's hesitation.

"Dear Lumi," he said softly, "Let your light shine before others, that they may see your good deeds and feel grateful for the light in the world."

Lumi was unsure. "But what if they don't like my light? What if it's too bright?"

Elder Willow answered, "Your light is a gift, meant to illuminate the darkness. Don't hide it away; let it guide, inspire, and warm the hearts of those who witness it."

Taking Elder Willow's words to heart, Lumi made a decision.

That night, she flew out from her leafy hideaway.

As she soared through the sky, her glow touched everything it passed. The darkened flowers bloomed in her light, the lost critters found their way, and her radiance even made a young sapling sprout its first leaf.

Everyone was amazed by the night of wonders Lumi had created. They gathered around Elder Willow, singing praises and thanking the heavens for the blessings of light and love.

"Look, Lumi," said Elder Willow, "your good deeds have led them to feel a greater appreciation for the beauty and goodness of life. They are praising the essence of love and kindness, the true light in the heavens."

Lumi finally understood. Her light was not just for her; it was a reflection of something much greater, something divine that connected all living things.

From that day on, Lumi the Firefly never hid her light. She let it shine brightly, touching the lives of all who lived in Whispering Woods.

And so, the forest creatures learned that each of them had their own unique light, a gift to share with the world, illuminating the path for others to find their way.

"Let your light shine before men, that they may see your good deeds and praise your Father in heaven."

Whisper the Owl and the Hidden Sanctuary

IN THE SERENE MEADOWS of Tranquil Grove, lived Whisper, a wise owl known for her depth and understanding.

Many animals would approach Whisper for advice and counsel, and she was always happy to help. However, they started noticing something peculiar: Whisper would frequently disappear to a secluded place, a hidden sanctuary known to none.

One day, Sage, a young squirrel, couldn't hold his curiosity anymore.

"Why do you go away so often, Whisper? Are you seeking some secret treasure?"

Whisper smiled and recalled the teachings of Grand Elder, the oldest tree in Tranquil Grove: "But when you find your inner wisdom, go into your sanctuary, close the door and speak to the unseen wisdom that connects us all. Then, the unseen wisdom that knows what is done in secret will reward you."

Sage was intrigued but puzzled.

"How does that work? What's this secret treasure you find?"

Whisper felt it was time to share her understanding: "The treasure is not material, Sage. It's the peace, clarity, and wisdom I find when I disconnect from the world to connect with something greater."

Inspired, Sage decided to give it a try.

He found a quiet corner underneath a large maple leaf, closed his eyes, and focused. At first, he felt a little silly, but gradually he found his thoughts clearing, his heart feeling lighter.

Days passed, and Sage realized he was happier, kinder, and more patient. Others started noticing it too. But like Whisper, he kept his sanctuary a secret.

Soon, the forest began to sense the change.

Plants seemed to flourish around Sage's secret spot, and animals that interacted with him felt a newfound sense of peace and warmth. Sage was amazed; he felt rewarded but not in a way he could see or touch—it was a reward he felt deep within.

Whisper sensed the change in Sage and called him over.

"You've found it, haven't you? The hidden treasure," she said with twinkling eyes.

"I have," Sage replied, his heart full of gratitude. "And I understand now why it's a treasure best kept secret."

Whisper nodded, pleased that the cycle of wisdom would continue through new stewards like Sage.

And so, Whisper and Sage continued to nurture their hidden sanctuaries, reaping rewards not of this world but of a place deep within, where true treasure lies.

The animals of Tranquil Grove may not have known why Whisper and Sage were so wise and serene, but they felt the invisible blessings that seemed to emanate from them, creating a cycle of goodness that touched every life they met.

"But when you pray, go into your room, close the door and pray to your Father, who is unseen. Then your Father who sees what is done in secret will reward you."

Gentle Grace the Rabbit and the Cycle of Forgiveness

IN THE FIELDS OF SERENITY Meadow, where daisies danced and willows whispered, lived Gentle Grace, a warm-hearted rabbit.

Grace was known for her kindness and her ability to see the good in others. However, her trusting nature was sometimes taken advantage of.

One day, Sneaky Sly the Fox did something regrettable.

Sly, driven by his hunger and impulsive nature, raided Grace's carefully gathered stash of food. When Grace discovered this, her heart sank.

Elder Blossom, a wise, old oak tree, felt the pain of the meadow and beckoned Grace over.

"Something troubling has happened, hasn't it?" Elder Blossom asked.

Grace nodded, holding back tears, "Sly took all my food. What should I do?"

Elder Blossom offered these words, "If you forgive others when they wrong you, the unseen goodness that watches over us will also forgive you."

Grace pondered deeply. "Forgive Sly? After what he did?"

"Forgiveness doesn't make what Sly did right," Elder Blossom explained, "but it sets your own heart free and opens the way for kindness to return to you."

Taking a deep breath, Grace felt a strong sense of purpose fill her. She decided to forgive Sly.

The next day, Grace approached Sly with a small offering of berries.

"I forgive you, Sly, for what you did. And I hope you learn the value of kindness and sharing," she said softly, placing the berries before him.

Sly looked stunned. No one had ever shown him such forgiveness and grace.

Over the next few weeks, something miraculous happened.

Touched by Grace's forgiveness, Sly began to change. He became more thoughtful and shared food with others. And as if by some unseen magic, Grace's stash replenished itself, fuller and richer than before.

Elder Blossom noticed the transformation in both Grace and Sly and called them over.

"See the power of forgiveness? Grace, your kindness has not only come back to you but has also transformed Sly. And Sly, the forgiveness you received has become your path to redemption."

Both nodded, their eyes meeting in a newfound understanding and respect.

Grace felt the weight of resentment lifted from her heart, replaced by a profound peace.

Sly, who had been given a second chance, vowed never to betray the trust of others again. In turn, he also learned to forgive, continuing the cycle that Grace had started.

And so, the animals of Serenity Meadow lived harmoniously, guided by the wisdom that forgiveness is not just an act but a powerful cycle that heals and transforms.

"If you forgive men when they sin against you, your heavenly Father will also forgive you."

The Weighty Wisdom Scrolls

IN THE MAGICAL VILLAGE of Booklandia, there lived experts known as the WisdomKeepers. They were the guardians of the Great Library, a building that held scrolls of wisdom accumulated over centuries. People came from all over the world to study and learn from these scrolls.

The WisdomKeepers prided themselves on their expertise. They spent their days reading and interpreting the ancient scrolls, creating an intricate set of rules and guidelines known as "The Weighty Wisdom." They believed that everyone should follow these rules to live a meaningful life.

But there was a problem. The WisdomKeepers made the rules so complicated that people struggled to understand them. Even worse, they would add more and more guidelines every week, until the Weighty Wisdom became an enormous, heavy scroll that no one could carry or read easily.

One day, a young girl named Emily came to Booklandia. She was excited to learn but became disheartened when she saw the massive Weighty Wisdom scroll. "How can I ever understand all of this?" she wondered.

Just then, Tim, a curious squirrel who loved reading, scurried by and noticed Emily's concern. Tim had observed the WisdomKeepers and their rules for quite some time and had his own thoughts about it.

"Hold on, young one!" Tim chattered. "Don't you see? The WisdomKeepers are making life difficult for everyone. They burden you with rules that even they don't understand entirely! And when you struggle, they won't even lift a paw—uh, I mean, a finger—to help!"

Emily thought about it and realized Tim was right. Armed with her newfound clarity, she went to the Great Library and stood before the WisdomKeepers.

"And you experts in the law," Emily bravely proclaimed, "woe to you! You've made these scrolls so weighty that no one can carry them, yet you do nothing to lighten the load!"

Her words resonated in the Great Library like an echoing gong. The WisdomKeepers looked at each other, their faces flushed with embarrassment. For the first time, they began to see the burden they had placed on the people of Booklandia.

From that day on, the WisdomKeepers vowed to simplify the rules and offer help to anyone who sought wisdom. They rewrote the Weighty Wisdom into a much shorter, more understandable "Pocket Wisdom" that people could easily read and carry.

Emily, Tim, and the rest of Booklandia celebrated this change, and people finally felt free to learn and grow without being weighed down by confusing rules.

And so, the Great Library became a place of true wisdom, where learning was a joy, and carrying the weight of wisdom was a burden no more.

"And you experts in the law, woe to you, because you load people down with burdens they can hardly carry, and you yourselves will not lift one finger to help them."

Time-Ticking Toby the Turtle and the Hourglass Lake

DEEP IN THE TRANQUIL forest of Winding Woods, a sparkling lake shimmered like a mirror reflecting the sky. Around this lake, known as Hourglass Lake, lived Time-Ticking Toby, a turtle obsessed with time.

Toby had a habit: he'd swim around the lake every day, counting each tick of time that passed, always worrying about losing time or not having enough of it.

One day, Elder Willow, the wise tree overlooking the lake, spoke to Toby.

"Who of you by worrying can add a single hour to his life?" said Elder Willow, his branches swaying gently in the wind.

Toby looked up, startled. "What do you mean, Elder Willow? Time is all we have!"

Elder Willow sighed and invited Toby to take a closer look at the lake.

"Look into the water, Toby. What do you see?"

Toby stared at the lake's surface and saw his own reflection, but also the fleeting clouds and the dancing sunbeams. "I see life passing by," he said softly.

"Exactly," said Elder Willow, "Life is happening now, and by worrying about time, you miss the beauty of each moment."

Toby felt a pang of realization. "So, what should I do?"

"Live, Toby, live! Take each moment as it comes and realize that the present is the only time that truly belongs to you," Elder Willow advised.

Toby thought about it. Could he really let go of his obsession with time? Could he learn to live in the present?

Taking a deep breath, Toby decided to give it a try.

For the first time in ages, he swam leisurely in the lake, basking in the sun's warmth and enjoying the gentle ripples of the water. He chatted with dragonflies, watched the fish play, and felt the lake's calm embrace.

And, for the first time, he wasn't worried about how long each joy would last.

That evening, Toby felt different—refreshed and truly alive.

He returned to Elder Willow, his heart filled with gratitude. "You were right. I couldn't add a single hour to my life by worrying, but I added life to my hours by living them."

Elder Willow nodded with satisfaction.

"Ah, Toby, you've grasped a timeless truth. Life isn't measured by the number of ticks on a clock but by the moments that take our breath away."

And so, Time-Ticking Toby became Timeless Toby, a turtle who still respected time but no longer let it dictate his life. He became a living reminder that no amount of worry can add time to life, but living fully can certainly add life to time.

"Who of you by worrying can add a single hour to his life?"

Tomorrow-Tina the Rabbit and the Magical Meadow

IN THE CHARMING WOODLAND of Evergreen Grove, where flowers bobbed their heads in greeting and trees whispered ancient tales, lived Tomorrow-Tina, a rabbit who was always fretting about the future.

"Will it rain tomorrow? Will I find enough food? What if something bad happens?" These were the thoughts that constantly buzzed in her mind.

Grandma Sage, the eldest rabbit in the Grove, noticed Tina's endless worrying.

One sunny afternoon, Grandma Sage called Tina over and said, "Do not worry about tomorrow, for tomorrow will worry about itself. Each day has enough trouble of its own."

Tina twitched her ears skeptically. "But Grandma Sage, how can we prepare for the future if we don't worry about it?"

Grandma Sage led Tina to the edge of a blooming meadow.

"Look around, Tina. This meadow is magical; it blossoms every day but only lasts until sunset. If you spend all day worrying about tomorrow's blossoms, you'll miss the beauty that's right in front of you."

Intrigued, Tina decided to spend the day exploring the magical meadow.

She sniffed the fragrant flowers, nibbled on the tender grass, and basked in the warm sun. To her surprise, she felt her worries slowly melt away. For the first time, Tina found herself fully immersed in the joy of the present moment.

That night, a light rain showered Evergreen Grove.

The next morning, the magical meadow was even more vibrant than before, just as Grandma Sage had subtly hinted.

Overwhelmed with happiness, Tina hopped back to Grandma Sage. "You were right! By not worrying about tomorrow, I got to enjoy today, and the meadow still bloomed beautifully the next day."

Grandma Sage chuckled and nuzzled Tina lovingly.

"You see, my dear, each day comes with its own set of challenges and blessings. Worrying about tomorrow not only ruins today but also clouds your ability to cope with the future."

From that day on, Tomorrow-Tina became Today-Tina, a rabbit who still thought about the future but never at the expense of the present. She became a joyful reminder to all of Evergreen Grove that each day truly has enough trouble—and enough beauty—of its own.

"Do not worry about tomorrow, for tomorrow will worry about itself. Each day has enough trouble of its own."

Judgy Jack the Squirrel and the Mirror Pond

IN THE SERENE AND FRIENDLY realm of Nutwood Forest, where trees stood tall like wise elders and streams sang lullabies, lived Judgy Jack, a squirrel with a peculiar habit—he loved to judge others.

"Too slow," he'd snicker at Sammy the Snail.

"Too loud," he'd complain about Chirpy Carol the Sparrow.

"Too clumsy," he'd smirk at Wobbly Wendy the Deer.

Wise Oak, the oldest tree in the forest, noticed Jack's constant judgments.

One day, as Jack was critiquing the way Petal the Butterfly fluttered, Wise Oak interrupted, "Do not judge, or you too will be judged."

Jack twitched his bushy tail dismissively. "Why should I worry? I'm just stating the obvious."

"Come with me," said Wise Oak.

With a wave of his mighty branch, Wise Oak unveiled a secret pond, its surface as still as glass. "It's called the Mirror Pond. Take a look."

When Jack peered into the water, he saw not just his reflection but also vignettes from his own life—times when he was slow, loud, and even clumsy. Each scene was accompanied by the same judgments he had passed onto others.

Astonished and humbled, Jack turned to Wise Oak.

"I see now that I've been far from perfect. Why did the pond show me these things?"

Wise Oak rustled his leaves gently. "The Mirror Pond reflects not just your face but your heart and actions. It shows you how your judgments circle back to you, like ripples in water."

Realizing the wisdom in Wise Oak's words, Jack felt a wave of regret wash over him.

"What can I do to make amends?"

"Start by appreciating others for who they are. Instead of focusing on their flaws, celebrate their uniqueness," suggested Wise Oak.

Inspired to change, Jack spent the next days observing and appreciating the qualities in others that he had once judged.

He cheered on Sammy the Snail for his perseverance, admired Chirpy Carol for her cheerful tunes, and found beauty in Wobbly Wendy's uncoordinated dance through the meadow.

As he let go of his judgments, something magical happened. The forest seemed brighter, the songs sweeter, and life itself more enjoyable.

Finally, Jack returned to the Mirror Pond.

This time, the pond showed him embracing all the creatures he had previously judged, and in the end, it showed a joyful, peaceful Jack.

Overwhelmed, Jack thanked Wise Oak.

"Your wisdom has set me free from my own judgments," he said, feeling truly enlightened.

"And in doing so, you've set others free to be themselves. Always remember, Jack, judgment distances you from others, but understanding brings you closer."

From that day on, Judgy Jack became Joyful Jack, a squirrel who celebrated the diversity and beauty in everyone. And Nutwood Forest was all the better for it, reminding every creature that lived within it that judgment is but a mirror reflecting the judge.

"Do not judge, or you too will be judged."

Specky Spencer the Hedgehog and the Forest of Mirrors

IN THE HEART OF WHISPERING Woods, where trees held secrets and brooks told tales, lived Specky Spencer, a hedgehog who had an uncanny knack for spotting the tiniest flaws in everyone else.

"Your feathers are uneven," he'd tell Tina the Peacock.

"Your web has a hole," he'd say to Wendy the Spider.

"Your song is off-key," he'd comment to Harmon the Songbird.

Old Maple, the wisest tree in the forest, had been observing Spencer's behavior.

"Why do you look at the speck of sawdust in your brother's eye and pay no attention to the plank in your own eye?" Old Maple questioned one day, after Spencer had just told Rocky the Racoon that his stripes were misaligned.

"What plank?" Spencer looked puzzled. "I'm just good at noticing details. It's helpful, isn't it?"

Old Maple gestured with a leafy branch towards a clearing that housed the Forest of Mirrors. "Why don't you take a stroll there?"

Intrigued, Spencer waddled to the clearing.

As he entered, mirrors appeared among the trees, reflecting not just his spiky exterior but also his inner world. The first mirror showed him making his critical remarks to his forest friends. The next mirror zoomed in on his own quills—some were bent, some were short, and some were missing altogether.

Stunned, Spencer finally saw the 'plank' in his own eye.

He felt his cheeks flush with embarrassment. How had he missed his own imperfections while pointing out the tiny flaws in others?

Ashamed yet enlightened, Spencer returned to Old Maple.

"You were right," he said softly. "I was so focused on the sawdust in others' eyes that I ignored the plank in my own."

Old Maple's leaves rustled gently, like a soft applause.

"Ah, Spencer. Sometimes the hardest thing to see is what's in ourselves. The lesson here is not just to refrain from judging others, but also to turn that discerning eye inward for self-improvement."

Invigorated by his newfound insight, Spencer began to change.

He still noticed details, but instead of using them to critique, he used them to help. He advised Tina on how to groom her feathers, helped Wendy repair her web, and encouraged Harmon to practice his tunes. And in the process, he became more aware and accepting of his own flaws.

Eventually, Spencer returned to the Forest of Mirrors.

This time, the mirrors reflected a hedgehog filled with compassion, understanding, and humility—both towards himself and others.

And so, Specky Spencer became Soulful Spencer, a hedgehog who realized that the path to a harmonious life lay not in pointing out specks in others but in acknowledging and addressing the planks in ourselves.

"Why do you look at the speck in of sawdust in your brother's eye and pay no attention to the plank in your own eye?"

Wishing Willow the Fox and the Three Magic Trees

IN THE MYSTICAL FOREST of Enchanted Pines, where moonbeams danced and stars twinkled, lived Wishing Willow, a young fox full of curiosity but also ridden with questions and uncertainties.

"I wonder where I can find the sweetest berries," she pondered.

"How do I become the swiftest runner in the forest?"

"Is there a way to be wise like Elder Owl?"

Wise Elder Owl, who had been observing Willow's contemplations, softly hooted, "Ask and it will be given to you; seek and you will find; knock and the door will be opened to you."

Willow's ears perked up. "What do you mean, Elder Owl?"

"Deep in this forest are the Three Magic Trees—Tree of Knowledge, Tree of Skill, and Tree of Wisdom. They may have the answers you seek."

Intrigued, Willow decided to embark on a quest to find the Three Magic Trees.

First, she came across the Tree of Knowledge.

With a little hesitation, she asked, "Where can I find the sweetest berries?"

The tree shimmered, and its leaves turned into a map, leading her to a hidden berry patch. Delighted, Willow found the berries were indeed the sweetest she'd ever tasted.

Next, she found the Tree of Skill.

Feeling bolder, she inquired, "How can I become the swiftest runner?"

The tree's bark transformed into a set of exercise and training instructions. Willow followed them diligently and soon became faster than she had ever been.

Finally, she reached the Tree of Wisdom.

Taking a deep breath, she asked, "How can I become wise like Elder Owl?"

The tree glowed in a soft light, and a small book dropped from its branches. It was a journal. "Wisdom comes from self-reflection and experience. Use this journal to write down your thoughts, questions, and lessons from each day," said a voice from the tree.

Feeling grateful and empowered, Willow returned to Elder Owl.

"I've found the sweetest berries, learned to run swiftly, and received a journal for gaining wisdom. Your advice was perfect!"

Elder Owl hooted in approval. "You've learned that the world is abundant with opportunities and answers. You just need the courage to ask, seek, and knock. Remember, Willow, life unfolds when you take that first step of curiosity."

From then on, Wishing Willow was not just a dreamer but also a seeker. And in her journey, she found not just berries, speed, or wisdom but the true magic of life itself.

"Ask and it will be given to you; seek and you will find; knock and the door will be opened to you."

Gifty Gabby the Rabbit and the Generous Sky

IN THE SNUG BURROW of Blossom Meadow, lived Gifty Gabby, a rabbit known for her generous spirit. She delighted in gifting little presents to her young ones—soft leaves, colorful pebbles, and sweet-smelling flowers.

Yet, Gabby often worried about bigger gifts like safety from predators, abundant food for winter, and wisdom to guide her little ones.

Old Willow, the wise tree at the heart of Blossom Meadow, overheard Gabby's thoughts one day.

He gently whispered, "If you, then, though you are just a rabbit, know how to give good gifts to your children, how much more will your Father in the sky give good gifts to those who ask him!"

Intrigued, Gabby tilted her ears. "Father in the sky? Do you mean the sky can give gifts too?"

"Yes," replied Old Willow, "The sky, or as some say, the 'Father in Heaven,' is bountiful and loving. It showers rain for crops, offers sun for warmth, and gives stars for guidance. All you have to do is ask."

Inspired, Gabby sat in a quiet corner of her burrow that evening.

With a humble heart, she asked the sky for protection, food, and wisdom. As she spoke, she felt a wave of comfort envelop her.

The very next day, something magical happened.

A thick bush with thorny vines sprouted near her burrow, offering a natural barrier against predators. Soon after, she discovered a large patch of delicious, nutritious clovers—just in time for storing winter food.

Gabby was grateful but wondered about her request for wisdom.

That's when Little Timmy, her youngest, came running with a shiny pebble. "Look, Mom, the prettiest rock!"

Instead of just admiring it, Gabby seized the moment to teach him a life lesson. "Yes, it's beautiful, Timmy. Just like this pebble, you too have inner qualities that make you unique and special."

Suddenly, it hit her. Wisdom was not just something to be granted; it was to be discovered and shared through daily experiences.

Elated, she returned to Old Willow to share her joy and realizations.

Old Willow nodded sagely, "You see, Gabby, the gifts from the sky are often like seeds. They sprout, grow, and yield fruit when you nurture them with love, attention, and gratitude."

From that day on, Gifty Gabby never doubted the abundance and generosity of the 'Father in the sky.' She continued to give good gifts to her little ones, and she knew that much greater gifts were always waiting for those who sincerely ask.

"If you, then, though you are evil, know how to give good gifts to your children, how much more will your Father in heaven give good gifts to those who ask him!"

Tumbles the Rabbit and the Power of Forgiveness

IN THE COZY GLEN OF Graceful Gardens lived Tumbles the Rabbit, known for his adventurous spirit but also for his clumsy ways.

Tumbles loved exploring, but his curiosity often led to mishaps. One day, while digging near Old Willow, Tumbles accidentally disturbed the roots, causing the tree to lose many of its leaves.

The forest creatures were upset. Old Willow was not just any tree; it was home to numerous birds and a symbol of wisdom and strength for the community.

Feeling guilty, Tumbles withdrew from everyone, unable to face the friends he had disappointed.

He hid in his burrow, drowning in his own guilt and shame. He remembered the solemn saying, "Take heart son, your sins are forgiven," but couldn't help but think, "Could I ever be forgiven for what I've done?"

Elder Elma, a wise old elephant, sensed Tumbles' sorrow and visited him.

"Tumbles, why are you hiding? Mistakes are part of life. The important thing is to acknowledge them and seek to make amends."

"But how can anyone forgive me?" Tumbles asked, his eyes welling with tears.

Elder Elma softly replied, "Take heart son, your sins are forgiven. What's crucial now is how you'll make it right."

Inspired by Elder Elma's words, Tumbles knew he had to act.

He approached Old Willow and, with the help of his friends, started repairing the disrupted roots. It was hard work, but Tumbles was committed. Slowly, the tree regained its vigor, and the leaves began to sprout anew.

Tumbles didn't stop there. He went on to build little wooden perches for the birds who had lost their homes, ensuring they had a place to rest.

Seeing his genuine efforts, the community forgave him, and Tumbles felt an immense weight lift from his shoulders.

He thanked Elder Elma, who simply said, "You've learned the essence of forgiveness—both receiving it and giving it. This will make you wiser and stronger than before."

From that day on, Tumbles still went on his little adventures, but he was more careful, more mindful, and above all, more forgiving—of both himself and others around him.

And so, Tumbles the Rabbit discovered that forgiveness was a gift, not just to be received but also to be given, for it is in forgiving that we find true peace and happiness.

"Take heart son, your sins are forgiven."

Sparrow the Selfless and the Cycle of Giving

IN A QUIET FOREST LIVED Sparrow, a tiny bird with a huge heart. Sparrow was an inquisitive soul, often exploring the far reaches of the forest and beyond.

One day, Sparrow came upon a beautiful flower that shimmered in the sunlight. "If I take this flower back to my nest, it will make my life so much more beautiful," thought Sparrow.

But just then, he saw a lonely caterpillar who seemed to be struggling to find food. The caterpillar looked up at the flower and sighed.

Sparrow was caught in a dilemma.

He could take the flower and enrich his own life, or leave it for the caterpillar who seemed to need it more. Sparrow recalled a wise saying: "Whoever finds his life will lose it, and whoever loses his life for my sake will find it."

Understanding the profound meaning behind these words, Sparrow decided to leave the flower for the caterpillar.

The caterpillar was elated and consumed the flower's leaves, eventually transforming into a beautiful butterfly.

Thankful, the butterfly visited Sparrow's nest one day with a gift—a cluster of seeds. "Plant these, and something special will grow," said the butterfly before fluttering away.

Curious, Sparrow planted the seeds near his nest. With time, the seeds grew into a radiant bush full of vibrant flowers, attracting all kinds of animals and insects. Sparrow's corner of the forest became a sanctuary of beauty and life.

Not only did Sparrow receive more beauty than he gave up, but he also gained friendships and a lively community around him.

One day, Sparrow found himself sitting on a branch of the flower bush, contemplating his decision from long ago. "I gave up a single flower but gained a whole garden, and not just for me, but for everyone," he thought, grateful and fulfilled.

The other creatures, noticing Sparrow's wisdom and selflessness, started to follow his example.

In helping each other, they found that they didn't lose anything; rather, they gained a richer life. The forest became a haven of sharing and compassion, all because Sparrow chose to give up something small for the greater good.

And so, Sparrow the Selfless lived a fulfilling life, surrounded by friends and enveloped by the beauty he had helped nurture.

He had truly found his life by giving it away, teaching everyone that the cycle of giving not only enriches the world around us but also brings unparalleled joy and fulfillment.

"Whoever finds his life will lose it, and whoever loses his life for my sake will find it."

Gentle Greta the Giraffe and the Tree of Tranquility

IN A LUSH SAVANNA, with sprawling landscapes and towering trees, lived Gentle Greta, a wise and nurturing giraffe. She was beloved for her kindness and the comfort she offered to those around her.

Close to Greta's home stood the Tree of Tranquility, a majestic tree with branches that reached towards the sky and roots that dug deep into the earth. Many believed this tree had magical qualities, as anyone who spent time under its branches felt their troubles drift away.

Greta, being the caretaker of the Tree of Tranquility, had one simple rule: "Come to me, all you who are weary and burdened, and I will give you rest."

One by one, animals of all sizes came to sit under the tree, sharing their worries and heartaches with Greta. With a soothing voice and a compassionate heart, Greta would guide them into the shade of the tree, allowing them to feel its calming energies.

Zara the Zebra was one such visitor.

Tired from constantly running away from predators and weary from the harsh life of the savanna, Zara arrived at the Tree of Tranquility. Greta welcomed her with open arms.

"Rest your stripes, dear Zara," Greta said softly, "and let the Tree of Tranquility take away your burdens."

Zara did as she was told and felt an immediate sense of peace wash over her.

Weeks passed, and the word spread. Animals from far and wide visited the Tree of Tranquility, each finding solace and peace under its shade and through Greta's kind words.

Even the fiercest of lions and the most anxious of meerkats found their way there, and each left feeling lighter, shedding the weight of their worries and fears.

As time passed, something extraordinary happened.

The tree began to grow taller and more magnificent, its branches becoming sturdier and its leaves more vibrant. The animals realized that their collective peace and goodwill were feeding the tree, making it stronger and even more tranquil.

Greta smiled, understanding the beautiful cycle of giving and receiving. "You see, dear friends, in seeking rest for yourselves, you've also given rest and strength to this wonderful tree. Your peace has been its nourishment."

And so, the Tree of Tranquility became a living testament to the power of sharing burdens and finding peace.

Animals continued to visit, each contributing to the tree's magic, and each finding their own peace in return.

Greta, standing tall beside the tree, remained a beacon of hope and solace, ever inviting and ever kind, reminding all that it's okay to seek help when weary and burdened.

"Come to me, all you who are weary and burdened, and I will give you rest."

Timely Tina the Apple Tree and the Orchard of Choices

IN THE ORCHARD OF CHOICES, trees of all kinds stretched as far as the eye could see. Each tree had its own unique characteristics, but none were as peculiar as Timely Tina, an apple tree.

Tina was not an ordinary apple tree; she had the unique ability to produce either sweet or sour apples, depending on how she was treated.

The animal community had a saying: "Make a tree good and its fruit will be good, or make a tree bad and its fruit will be bad, for a tree is recognized by its fruit."

Tina took this saying to heart. She knew that the kind of fruit she produced would reflect the care she received and the values she upheld.

One year, the birds and critters were particularly kind to Tina.

They pruned her branches, watered her roots, and kept her free from pests. True to the saying, Tina produced the sweetest apples that season, enjoyed by all.

However, the following year brought new challenges.

Droughts plagued the Orchard of Choices, and tensions among the animals grew. A few began to ignore Tina, and some even threw rocks at her out of frustration. That year, Tina's apples were sour and unpalatable, reflecting the neglect and negative energy she had received.

The Wise Owl, who was respected by all in the Orchard, decided it was time for a community gathering.

Gathering all the animals under Tina's shade, Wise Owl pointed to Tina's sour apples and recounted the saying: "Remember, a tree is recognized by its fruit. What do these sour apples say about us as a community?"

The animals hung their heads in shame, recognizing their shortcomings.

The young squirrel, Sally, spoke up.

"I think it's time we treat Tina, and each other, with the kindness and respect we all deserve. Only then can we enjoy sweet fruit again."

Wise Owl nodded in agreement. "Well said, Sally. It starts with making the tree good."

From that day on, the animals pledged to treat not just Tina but all trees in the Orchard of Choices with kindness and care.

The following year, Tina was back to producing the sweetest apples, her fruit reflecting the renewed harmony and goodwill in the community.

Each bite of her apples served as a reminder to the animals.

It reminded them that the goodness or badness of a tree's fruit is a collective reflection of the community's values and actions. And so, they all lived harmoniously, understanding the profound wisdom in recognizing a tree by its fruit.

"Make a tree good and its fruit will be good, or make a tree bad and its fruit will be bad, for a tree is recognized by its fruit."

Furry Fred and the Family of Goodwill

DEEP IN THE LUSH FOREST of Harmony, lived a small raccoon named Furry Fred. Though Fred was often mischievous and playful, he had a deep sense of right and wrong.

Fred had always wondered what it meant to have a family. He had been orphaned at a young age and grew up all by himself. However, the wise old turtle, Tim, shared an ancient saying with him: "For whoever does the will of my Father in heaven is my brother and sister and mother."

Fred was puzzled. "How can someone who isn't related to me become my family?" he thought.

Tim saw the confusion in Fred's eyes and explained.

"In the forest of Harmony, doing good deeds and helping each other is considered the will of the Father. Whoever does good is family, no matter their shape or size."

Inspired, Fred made a decision. He would make it his mission to be kind, help others, and by doing so, find his 'family.'

Fred's first chance came sooner than he expected.

A wildfire broke out at the far end of the forest. Fred, remembering the wise words, instantly began to dig small trenches to stop the fire from spreading.

Fiona the Fox saw Fred's courage and joined in. Together, they managed to save a portion of the forest.

A few days later, Fred came across Dana the Deer, stuck in a trap.

Without a second thought, Fred used his nimble fingers to free her. Dana thanked him and looked at him with newfound respect. "You are like the brother I never had," she said.

Fred felt his heart swell with joy. He was beginning to understand what Tim meant.

As days turned into months, Fred found himself involved in more acts of goodwill and kindness.

He helped Benny the Bird build a new nest after a storm, guided lost butterflies back to their group, and even taught young animals how to find food safely.

Soon enough, animals began to regard him as family—a brother to some, a son to others, and even a caring friend to many.

One fine day, Fred found himself surrounded by all the animals he had helped.

They threw him a surprise 'Family Day' celebration under the largest tree in the forest. It was a joyful gathering, full of laughter, sharing, and gratitude.

As Fred looked around, he realized that he had indeed found his family—a family not connected by birth, but by goodwill and kind deeds.

Tim the turtle ambled up to Fred and said, "You see, Fred, you are a living example of the saying. You did the will of the Father, and now look at your family!"

Fred's eyes filled with tears of happiness.

He finally understood the wisdom of the saying: "For whoever does the will of my Father in heaven is my brother and sister and mother."

And from that day on, Fred lived happily, surrounded by his newfound family in the forest of Harmony.

"For whoever does the will of my Father in heaven is my brother and sister and mother."

Daring Danny and the Field of Hidden Wonders

IN THE QUAINT VILLAGE of Sunnyside, where people cherished simple joys and friendships, lived a curious boy named Daring Danny. Danny was known for his adventurous spirit and unquenchable curiosity. One fine afternoon, while playing in a seemingly ordinary field, he stumbled upon something extraordinary.

As Danny dug into the soil with his bare hands, he felt something hard and metallic. Eagerly, he unearthed a small, ornate box.

Danny opened the box and couldn't believe his eyes: it was filled with gemstones of all kinds—sapphires, rubies, and diamonds—each shining brighter than the last.

Remembering a parable his grandmother had once told him, Danny knew instantly what he had to do: "The kingdom of heaven is like treasure hidden in a field. When a man found it, he hid it again, and then in his joy went and sold all he had and bought that field."

Danny carefully reburied the box and raced home, his heart pounding with joy and anticipation.

He sold his favorite toy, a model airplane that could really fly, and even his beloved comic book collection. Using the money he gathered, Danny bought the field from Old Man Jenkins, the landowner, who couldn't believe his luck. After all, the field was not fertile and seemed to have no real value.

Danny couldn't wait any longer; he dug up the treasure once again, this time planning to use it wisely.

Instead of keeping it all for himself, he sold a few of the gems and used the money to build a playground in the field for all the village children to enjoy. He also planted fruit trees and vegetable gardens to feed the needy.

News of Danny's good deeds spread like wildfire, and soon people from all walks of life were coming to see the "Field of Hidden Wonders," as it had come to be known.

Some offered to help in maintaining the gardens, while others contributed books to start a small community library near the playground.

Old Man Jenkins, realizing the newfound value of what he'd considered a worthless piece of land, approached Danny with regret in his eyes.

"Young man, I had no idea what I was giving away. This field truly is magical."

Danny smiled, "The field was always just a field. The real treasure is what we make of it."

As years passed, the Field of Hidden Wonders became a sanctuary of joy, knowledge, and community.

People often said it was like a small piece of heaven on Earth. Danny knew he had discovered something far more valuable than gemstones; he had discovered the joy of creating a kingdom of goodness, right here in the heart of Sunnyside.

And so, Daring Danny grew up to be Wise Danny, forever cherishing the lesson of the hidden treasure. He understood that the true kingdom of heaven is not just about discovering treasure, but about what you do with it once it's found.

"The kingdom of heaven is like treasure hidden in a field. When a man found it, he hid it again, and then in his joy went and sold all he had and bought that field."

Mustard-Mary and the Moving Mountain

IN THE TRANQUIL VILLAGE of Hopeville, children played by the lake, people laughed in the market, and the towering Mount Grumble watched over all. But Mount Grumble had started to awaken, sending tremors that rippled through the village.

Terrified, the villagers decided they needed to move their entire village to the other side of the lake. The task seemed insurmountable. That was until Mustard-Mary, a young girl of incredible optimism but not much else, stood up.

"I think we can move the mountain," said Mustard-Mary confidently.

The villagers chuckled. "You're just a child," said Village Elder Vincent. "What do you know about moving mountains?"

Remembering words of wisdom she had heard, Mustard-Mary said, "Because you have so little faith. I tell you the truth, if you have faith as small as a mustard seed, you can say to this mountain, 'Move from here to there,' and it will move. Nothing is impossible for you."

Intrigued but skeptical, the villagers decided to humor her.

Mustard-Mary led them to the foot of Mount Grumble. Holding up a tiny mustard seed, she said, "See this seed? It's small, but it can grow into a sturdy tree. Our faith can do the same. Let's all focus our belief that Mount Grumble can be moved."

At first, nothing happened. But Mustard-Mary closed her eyes, held the mustard seed tightly, and chanted, "Move from here to there."

Suddenly, the earth trembled.

To everyone's astonishment, Mount Grumble began to shift—slowly and then more quickly, until it had moved far enough away to no longer pose a threat to Hopeville.

The villagers were amazed.

"Did we do that?" asked a carpenter.

"Was it magic?" wondered a teacher.

"No," said Mustard-Mary, "it was faith. Even if it's as tiny as this mustard seed, it can move mountains."

The people of Hopeville learned a valuable lesson that day.

They no longer doubted the power of faith, no matter how small. And they never forgot the courage of Mustard-Mary, the little girl who showed them that nothing was impossible if they believed.

From then on, they lived in peace, their homes safe and their faith unwavering, always remembering that even the smallest amount of faith could lead to the most miraculous outcomes.

"Because you have so little faith. I tell you the truth, if you have faith as small as a mustard seed, you can say to this mountain, 'Move from here to there' and it will move. Nothing is impossible for you."

Serene Sally and the Quiet Grove

IN THE BUSTLING MEADOW of Wildflower Valley, life never seemed to pause. Birds chirped constantly, rabbits frolicked about, and insects busily went about their day. Among them lived Serene Sally, a gentle rabbit who often felt overwhelmed by the ceaseless activity around her.

One day, a mysterious elder tortoise named Tilly arrived at the valley. "This place is so lively, yet it lacks tranquility," she observed.

Sally agreed, "It's as if no one knows how to take a break. Even I feel drained at times."

Tilly smiled softly, "Come with me by yourselves to a quiet place and get some rest."

Intrigued, Sally decided to follow Tilly.

They walked past the fields of singing crickets and darting butterflies, crossing a babbling brook, and finally reached a secluded grove. It was quiet, serene, and strangely comforting. The air was filled with the scent of pine and earth.

"Sit down and close your eyes," Tilly instructed.

Sally did as she was told.

For the first time in what felt like forever, she wasn't thinking about what to do next. She felt peaceful, her senses heightened yet relaxed. After some time, Tilly tapped her gently and said, "Let's go back."

As they returned, Sally felt recharged, carrying a new sense of calmness within her. She couldn't help but notice that the valley seemed less overwhelming, its vibrancy less draining.

Back in the valley, the other animals noticed the change in Sally.

"What happened to you?" asked Energetic Eddie, a local squirrel.

"I took a break," said Sally. "A real, peaceful break. And it has made all the difference."

Word spread like wildfire.

Soon, animals were coming to Sally, asking her to guide them to the quiet grove. And every time she returned, she would find Tilly waiting to welcome them.

Over time, the animals of Wildflower Valley learned to balance their bustling lives with moments of peace, all thanks to Serene Sally and her newfound friend, Tilly the Tortoise.

The valley was still a lively place, but it also became a valley of rest and tranquility, where every creature learned the value of taking a break.

"Come with me by yourselves to a quiet place and get some rest."

Lenny the Lamb and the Heart of the Meadow

IN THE VIBRANT MEADOW of Unity, animals of all kinds lived harmoniously. Lenny the Lamb, however, always felt something was missing. Though he had friends and family, he felt an urge to connect on a deeper level with the world around him.

One sunny day, Wise Wally the Owl flew down to perch next to Lenny. "You look lost," Wally said.

Lenny sighed, "I want to love more deeply, not just my friends and family, but everything."

Wally tilted his head thoughtfully, "Love the Lord your God with all your heart and with all your soul and with all your mind."

"How do I do that?" Lenny asked, puzzled.

"First, you must love with all your heart," said Wally, and led Lenny to Rosie the Rabbit, who was struggling to build a shelter.

Lenny felt compassion and immediately helped Rosie. His heart swelled with love as they completed the shelter together.

"Now, love with all your soul," Wally instructed.

Lenny was guided to a stream where Fishy Fred was trapped in a fishing net. Lenny jumped into the water and set Fred free. As Fred swam away, Lenny felt his soul connect deeply with the water and its creatures.

"Finally, love with all your mind," said Wally.

Wally took Lenny to the middle of the Meadow, where a mysterious, colorful stone stood. It was said that the stone held the spirit of the Meadow.

"Focus your thoughts on loving every particle of this world," said Wally.

Lenny closed his eyes, his mind filled with love and gratitude.

As he concentrated, the stone began to glow brighter and brighter, until its light encompassed the whole Meadow.

When he opened his eyes, Lenny felt connected to everything and everyone, as if they were all a part of him and he a part of them.

"You've done it, Lenny," said Wally, "You've learned to love with your heart, your soul, and your mind."

Lenny realized he felt complete. The missing piece he had been searching for was the deeper connection to the world around him.

From then on, Lenny became a beacon of love and unity in the Meadow.

The other animals were drawn to his wisdom and kindness. In learning to love deeply and completely, Lenny found his place in the grand tapestry of life, and the Meadow of Unity became even more united.

"Love the Lord your God will all your heart and with all your soul and with all your mind."

Timmy the Turtle and the Ripple of Love

IN THE TRANQUIL LAND of Emerald Pond, animals lived peacefully alongside each other. Timmy the Turtle was well-known for his wisdom and kindness. Yet, despite the harmony, Timmy sensed that everyone could be a little kinder to each other.

One day, Betty the Butterfly fluttered down next to him. "Timmy, why does it seem that we don't care as much for others as we do for ourselves?"

Timmy looked at her and said, "The key to a happier community is to love your neighbor as yourself."

"But how can we practice that?" Betty wondered aloud.

"Let's start small and watch the ripple effect," Timmy suggested.

The next morning, Timmy noticed Freddy the Frog struggling to catch flies for breakfast.

Instead of passing by, Timmy offered some of his own algae. "Here you go, Freddy. I had a good harvest this morning."

"Thank you, Timmy!" Freddy said, surprised and delighted.

Timmy then glided through the water to where Sammy the Snail was inching along the pond's edge.

"Would you like a lift, Sammy?" Timmy offered.

Sammy gratefully accepted and, with newfound speed, managed to reach his destination. "Wow, Timmy! I've never gotten anywhere this fast!"

Inspired by Timmy's actions, Betty decided to lend a helping wing herself.

She saw Penny the Pond Skater caught in some reeds. With a gentle push, Betty helped her out. "I saw Timmy helping others and thought I should too," said Betty.

Penny was so grateful that she then helped Benny the Beetle who had tipped over. Benny, in turn, assisted Cindy the Cricket who was stuck in a small hole.

The ripple effect of kindness spread through Emerald Pond like never before.

Soon, animals began not only looking out for themselves but also caring deeply for their neighbors. Helping each other became the new normal.

A week later, Timmy and Betty sat by the pond, watching the community flourish.

"See, Betty," Timmy said, "when you love your neighbor as yourself, a single act of kindness ripples through the pond, touching the lives of many."

Betty nodded, "I guess love really is the cornerstone of a happy community."

From then on, the inhabitants of Emerald Pond were not just neighbors but friends who looked out for each other, creating a haven of peace and love for all.

"Love your neighbor as yourself."

The Parable of Polly the Penguin and the Golden Fish

IN THE ICY LANDS OF Snowflake Valley lived Polly the Penguin, renowned for her wisdom and kindness. She helped fellow animals find food, gave advice, and always reminded them of the beauty of life.

One day, a shiny Golden Fish appeared in the valley's frozen pond. Whoever possessed the Golden Fish could wish for endless treasures. Soon, the animals of Snowflake Valley became obsessed with catching it.

Among them was Tommy the Seal, Polly's good friend. Tommy was never one for wealth or luxury, but the Golden Fish's allure captivated him.

Polly noticed the change in Tommy and the others. "Why is everyone acting so different?" she wondered.

A wise elder named Olaf the Owl told her, "No one can serve two masters. Either he will hate the one and love the other, or he will be devoted to the one and despise the other. You cannot serve both God and money."

The message struck Polly. She decided it was time for an intervention.

Gathering the animals around the frozen pond, Polly spoke, "Friends, remember what makes Snowflake Valley special—our love for each other and our joy in the little things. The Golden Fish may grant wishes, but it can't give us the happiness we give each other."

However, the Golden Fish suddenly surfaced, looking distressed.

"I am a cursed creature," said the Golden Fish. "I bring wealth, but I also bring unhappiness. Free me, and I can go back to being a regular fish, swimming happily with my family."

A silence fell over the crowd. Polly looked at Tommy, who finally seemed to awaken from his greed-driven daze.

Tommy approached the Golden Fish and gently freed it from the shallow water's edge, saying, "I choose to serve love and friendship, not wealth."

The Golden Fish shimmered and transformed into a simple, ordinary fish, swimming joyously back into the depths.

The animals cheered, their hearts lifted from the fog of greed and refocused on what truly mattered.

As the sun set that evening, Polly and Tommy sat by the pond. "Thank you, Polly, for reminding me of what's important," said Tommy.

Polly smiled, "And thank you, Tommy, for reminding us all that sometimes the choice between two masters is actually the choice between two lives. Choose wisely."

The animals of Snowflake Valley returned to their ways of love and community, forever cherishing the lesson that no one can serve two masters and that sometimes, the most valuable treasures are the ones you can't see.

"No one can serve two masters. Either he will hate the one and love the other, or he will be devoted to the one and despise the other. You cannot serve both God and money."

Tessa the Turtle and the Rowdy Rabbits

IN A SERENE FOREST called Greenfield Grove, Tessa the Turtle lived a quiet life, often spending her days meditating by the pond and helping animals in need. She was loved by many but misunderstood by a few.

Among those who didn't understand Tessa were the Rowdy Rabbits—three rambunctious siblings named Rita, Roger, and Rusty. They often played pranks on her, toppling her basket of berries or muddying the pond where she meditated.

One day, Tessa's friends asked, "Why don't you stand up to them? Why do you let them mistreat you?"

Tessa thought for a moment and replied, "But I tell you who hear me: Love your enemies, do good to those who hate you, bless those who curse you, pray for those who mistreat you."

Her friends were puzzled but respected her wisdom. The next morning, Tessa prepared baskets of fresh fruit and marched straight to the Rowdy Rabbits' burrow.

As she approached, Rita, Roger, and Rusty sprang out, ready to pounce. But when they saw Tessa carrying gifts, they paused.

"I've brought you these gifts as a token of peace and friendship," Tessa calmly stated.

Rita snickered, "Why would you do that? We've never been nice to you."

Tessa smiled, "Sometimes, understanding starts with a simple act of kindness. I hold no grudges. I only hope for peace among us."

One by one, the Rowdy Rabbits took a piece of fruit from the basket. As they tasted the sweet, juicy treats, something changed within them. It was as if the fruit carried Tessa's sincerity and kindness, melting the icy walls around their hearts.

Days passed, and the Rowdy Rabbits started to change their ways. They stopped their pranks and even began to help other animals. Tessa's kindness had sparked a transformation they never thought possible.

The other animals were amazed. "How did you do it?" they asked Tessa.

She smiled serenely, "In showing love where there was none, we open the doors to understanding and harmony."

And so, Tessa the Turtle and the Rowdy Rabbits became an example for all in Greenfield Grove, proving that even the toughest hearts could be softened by the potent power of kindness, love, and a little understanding.

"But I tell you who hear me: Love your enemies, do good to those who hate you, bless those who curse you, pray for those who mistreat you."

Generous Gina and the Forest's Gift

IN THE HEART OF THE enchanting Whispering Woods lived Generous Gina, a squirrel known for her endless kindness. Her treehouse was filled with acorns, berries, and all kinds of forest treasures, which she gladly shared with anyone who needed help.

One sunny day, Crafty Carl, a fox who had a reputation for taking more than he gave, sauntered into Gina's domain. "Hey Gina, heard you have some extra acorns. Mind if I take a few?"

Without a moment's hesitation, Gina welcomed him. "Of course, Carl! Give to everyone who asks you, that's my motto. Take what you need."

Carl grinned, taking more acorns than he actually needed, leaving the stash noticeably depleted.

Word spread through the forest about Carl's actions, and Gina's friends were outraged. "Gina, why did you let him take so much? You should demand your acorns back!"

Gina simply smiled, "If anyone takes what belongs to you, do not demand it back. The forest provides, and so will I."

As days passed, Gina continued her generous ways, sharing her remaining acorns and even helping to find new food sources. Soon, the stash was brimming again, thanks to the grateful animals who started contributing to it.

Meanwhile, Carl found that the acorns he had taken weren't sprouting. In fact, they seemed to lose their shine and vitality.

Realizing his mistake, Carl returned to Gina, his head hung low. "Gina, I need to apologize. I took more than I needed, and now these acorns are useless to me."

Gina looked at the lackluster acorns and then back at Carl. "The forest and its gifts thrive on the cycle of giving and kindness. When you break that cycle, the natural balance is disturbed."

Carl nodded, beginning to understand the wisdom in Gina's actions. "What should I do?"

"Start by giving," Gina said, handing him a single, vibrant acorn. "Take this and plant it. Nurture it, and when it bears fruit, share it with others."

Carl took the acorn, feeling its potential in the palm of his hand. As he planted and nurtured it, not only did the acorn sprout, but Carl himself started to change. He became a regular contributor to Gina's stash, ensuring that no one in the forest went hungry.

Years later, the forest was filled with trees that bore the most luscious acorns, all originating from the acorn Gina had given to Carl.

And so, Generous Gina and Crafty-turned-Caring Carl taught everyone in Whispering Woods a lesson that echoed through generations:

"In giving freely and not demanding back, we create a world of abundance and kindness for all."

"Give to everyone who asks you, and if anyone takes what belongs to you, do not demand it back."

Grandma Willow and the Orphaned Owlets

DEEP IN THE ENCHANTED Heartwood Forest lived Grandma Willow, an old and wise tree with sprawling branches that provided shade and solace to all who needed it. Grandma Willow was like a mother to the forest's inhabitants, always giving advice and sharing stories that had been passed down for generations.

One stormy evening, two orphaned owlets, Oliver and Olivia, were blown away from their home. Shivering and lost, they fluttered until they reached the nurturing canopy of Grandma Willow.

"Please, may we stay with you?" asked Oliver, his eyes brimming with tears.

"Of course, my little ones," Grandma Willow responded warmly. "Whoever welcomes one of these little children in my name welcomes me; and whoever welcomes me does not welcome me but the one who sent me."

The owlets found refuge in her sturdy branches, and as days passed, they listened to Grandma Willow's teachings, learning the values of kindness, compassion, and wisdom. They grew stronger and more confident.

Soon, word of Grandma Willow's new residents reached the heart of the forest. Some questioned why she would take in these orphaned owlets when she was already so old and had her branches full with other responsibilities.

"You already do so much for the forest, why take on more?" asked a curious deer.

Grandma Willow just chuckled, "When you welcome the vulnerable and the young into your life, you welcome the essence of life itself. By nurturing them, I am part of a cycle much larger than myself."

Time flew, and the owlets turned into wise and strong owls. They used the wisdom they gained from Grandma Willow to help other animals in need, continuing the legacy of kindness and compassion.

One day, the forest experienced a drought. The usually vibrant Heartwood Forest was parched, and water was scarce. During these tough times, Oliver and Olivia took turns flying long distances to bring water for Grandma Willow and the other forest inhabitants.

Seeing this, Grandma Willow shed tears of joy, nourishing the dry soil around her. "You've become the keepers of kindness, just as I hoped."

With the spirit of kindness and community, Heartwood Forest soon recovered from the drought, more united than ever.

Grandma Willow, Oliver, and Olivia became the epitome of what it means to welcome and nurture life in all its forms.

"For in welcoming the least among us, we welcome the grand scheme of life, the invisible hands that shape us, guide us, and make us who we are."

"Whoever welcomes one of these little children in my name welcomes me; and whoever welcomes me does not welcome me but the one who sent me."

Kindly Creek and the Village Children

IN THE GENTLE VILLAGE of Meadowgrove, there was a sparkling creek known as Kindly Creek. Its waters were clear, its ripples melodious, and it had an inexplicable sense of understanding. Kindly Creek was special, not just for its beauty, but for its wisdom.

Long ago, the creek was deemed off-limits for children by the village council. They believed that the young ones would be reckless, tarnishing the pristine waters and disturbing the peace.

But Kindly Creek thought differently.

"Let the little children come to me, and do not hinder them," the Creek would whisper when the wind blew through its reeds. "For the kingdom of God belongs to such as these."

One sunny morning, a young girl named Lily, tired of the strict rules, ventured near Kindly Creek. She sat down and started drawing on her sketchbook, capturing the shimmering water and the blooming wildflowers.

As she drew, she felt a warmth wash over her, as if the Creek itself was thanking her for her visit.

Soon, other children began to join her—Jack who loved to read, Timmy who liked to explore, and Sarah who enjoyed singing. Each child found a safe haven by Kindly Creek, engaging in activities that filled them with joy and peace.

When the village council found out, they were furious.

"These children should be kept away! They know nothing about preserving nature," argued Mr. Thorn, a member of the council.

But Elder Rose, the oldest in the village, spoke up, "Have you not seen? The Creek looks even more vibrant, and haven't you heard its joyful ripples? Maybe we should learn from the Creek and the children rather than keeping them apart."

The council members decided to visit Kindly Creek to see for themselves. Upon arrival, they were amazed. The Creek indeed looked happier, if such a thing were possible. Its waters were as clear as crystal, and its ripples seemed to be humming a happy tune.

The children were not harming the creek; they were enhancing its beauty by simply being themselves—innocent, joyful, and full of life.

Finally understanding the wisdom of Kindly Creek, the village council lifted the restrictions.

From that day on, the children were free to visit Kindly Creek. The creek, in return, continued to provide the children with life lessons of love, unity, and the sheer joy of existence.

And so, the village of Meadowgrove lived on, guided by the wisdom of a gentle creek and the pure hearts of its youngest residents.

"Let the little children come to me, and do not hinder them, for the kingdom of God belongs to such as these."

Humble Hill and the Door to the Sky

ONCE UPON A TIME, IN the little village of Tranquil Vale, there stood a peculiar hill called Humble Hill. It was not the tallest or the most beautiful hill, but it had a mysterious door embedded in its side, known as the Door to the Sky.

People from near and far would come to Humble Hill with golden keys, intricate puzzles, and complex theories, hoping to open the door. Many claimed they were wise enough to solve the mystery, but the door remained steadfast, as if mocking their futile attempts.

But, the hill had a secret.

"I tell you the truth, anyone who will not receive the kingdom of God like a little child will never enter it," Humble Hill would whisper when the evening breeze flowed through its grass.

One summer morning, a group of children from the village decided to play near Humble Hill. Among them was a young boy named Toby, who had always been fascinated by the tales of the Door to the Sky.

Unlike the adults who approached the door with determination and rigid focus, Toby stood before it with wide-eyed wonder, his heart filled with the innocence and curiosity of a child.

As he touched the door, something miraculous happened.

The door glowed and creaked open, unveiling a pathway filled with radiant light and celestial beauty. The other children watched in awe as the door accepted Toby's simple, childlike wonder as the key to its opening.

Amazed by the unfolding event, the villagers gathered around. The wise men and scholars couldn't believe their eyes; the door they had tried to unlock for years had easily opened for a child.

Elder Nora, the wisest among them, spoke, "Perhaps we've been approaching this all wrong. Toby didn't try to outsmart the door or solve a complex riddle. He simply stood before it as any child would—open-hearted, without pretense or arrogance. And the door, it seems, responded to that purity."

From that day on, the villagers began to understand the wisdom of Humble Hill.

They realized that sometimes wisdom comes in the simplest forms and that the kingdom of God is not just for the scholarly or the powerful but for those who carry a childlike innocence in their hearts.

From then on, every person, young and old, approached the door—and life itself—with a newfound humility and openness, much like a little child.

And the village of Tranquil Vale, guided by the wisdom of a humble hill, became a place of peace, unity, and boundless wonder.

"I tell you the truth, anyone who will not receive the kingdom of God like a little child will never enter it."

The Eternal Orchard

IN A KINGDOM FAR, FAR away, nestled between mighty mountains and lush valleys, lay an orchard known as the Eternal Orchard. It was said that the fruits from this orchard had the power to grant eternal life.

The king, a wise and loving ruler named King Valerian, cherished the orchard not for its fruit but for its profound significance. It was a gift from his late wife, Queen Serenity, and he considered it to be the heart and soul of the kingdom.

King Valerian had a single son, Prince Orion, who was destined to inherit the throne.

In a cruel twist of fate, the kingdom fell under a terrible curse that dried up rivers, withered crops, and weakened its people. The royal healers determined that the only way to break the curse was to use the fruit from the Eternal Orchard, but there was a catch: using the fruit would mean the orchard would never again bear its life-giving fruits.

The king was torn. The orchard was the last living memory of his beloved wife, but his people were suffering. After days of contemplation, King Valerian made a heartbreaking decision.

"For God so loved the world that he gave his one and only Son, that whoever believes in him shall not perish but have eternal life," King Valerian told Prince Orion, drawing upon an old scripture to explain his choice.

With a heavy heart, the king ordered the harvesting of the orchard's fruits to save his kingdom. When the people ate the fruit, the rivers began to flow, the crops flourished, and health returned to the people. The curse was broken.

Though the Eternal Orchard would never bear fruit again, its sacrifice was never forgotten. Prince Orion, deeply moved by his father's sacrifice, promised to be a ruler who would put the welfare of his people above all else.

Years passed, and Prince Orion became King Orion, a wise and loving ruler like his father. Under his rule, the kingdom flourished as it never had before. The people did not live forever, but they lived well, cherishing the love and sacrifices that had been made for them.

As for the Eternal Orchard, it became a sanctuary, a reminder of the unfathomable love that could save a world. Even without its life-giving fruits, the trees stood tall and proud, their empty branches a testament to a king's sacrifice and a love that was, indeed, eternal.

"For God so loved the world that he gave his one and only Son, that whoever believes in him shall not perish but have eternal life."

Little Finley and the Whispers of the Wind

IN THE MAGICAL VILLAGE of Greenwood, a young boy named Finley lived with his family. Finley was known for his infectious laugh and insatiable curiosity. But what set him apart was his ability to hear the "Whispers of the Wind," a gift from the Earth Mother to spread messages of love, kindness, and hope.

One sunny day, the wind began to whisper words Finley had never heard before:

"Go into all the world and preach the good news to all creation."

At first, Finley was puzzled. He was just a little boy; how could he go into all the world? But the whispers grew louder, and he knew he had to do something. He went to his parents and told them what he had heard.

His parents, wise and loving, told him, "Finley, sometimes the smallest voices can make the biggest impact. The world starts right here, in our village."

Feeling encouraged, Finley decided to start spreading the good news in Greenwood. He began by doing small acts of kindness. He helped Mrs. Willow, the elderly woman next door, with her garden. He read stories to the younger children in the village. He even shared his last piece of chocolate cake with his little sister, Freya.

Word began to spread throughout the village about Finley and his good deeds. Soon, others started joining him. They planted trees, helped repair broken homes, and took care of those who were sick. The entire village became a place of joy and community, all thanks to the message heard by a little boy.

Years later, Finley became a wise elder, but he never forgot the message from the Whispers of the Wind.

As an elder, he gathered the children around him and said, "Each one of you can spread good news, just like the wind spreads seeds. You don't have to travel the world; your world starts right here, with the people around you. Always remember, even the smallest voice can make the biggest impact."

And so, the children of Greenwood grew up with Finley's wisdom echoing in their hearts, and when they were old enough, they too heard the Whispers of the Wind, continuing to spread good news to all creation.

"Go into all the world and preach the good news to all creation."

Little Finley and the Cup of Choices

IN THE ENCHANTED VILLAGE of Greenwood, older Finley was now a wise elder. The Whispers of the Wind had brought him many messages over the years, guiding him and the villagers towards kindness and love. But one day, the wind whispered something that filled him with dread:

"Abba, Father, everything is possible for you. Take this cup from me. Yet not what I will, but what you will."

Finley knew that a time of great trial was coming. Fearing the unknown, he went to the oldest tree in the forest, a place where he often found comfort and wisdom.

"Old Tree, I've received a message that suggests a difficult path lies ahead. What should I do?"

The Old Tree rustled its leaves and said, "Finley, the Earth Mother gives each of us a cup to carry. Sometimes it's filled with joy, sometimes sorrow. Though you may wish to not drink from it, remember that life is a blend of both. What matters is how you accept it."

Finley nodded, his eyes wet with emotion. "Not what I will, but what you will," he whispered, echoing the words from the wind.

Returning to the village, Finley gathered everyone and shared the message from the Whispers of the Wind.

"Friends, a time of challenge may be upon us, but we will face it together. Each of us carries our own cup of choices and challenges, but it's how we drink from it that defines us," he said.

Days later, a severe storm hit Greenwood. Homes were damaged and crops were destroyed. Yet, the villagers worked together to rebuild and support one another. The trials were difficult, but the community's spirit was unbreakable.

Once the storm had passed and peace returned to Greenwood, everyone realized that the trials had brought them even closer. They were more grateful for what they had, and they treasured their community more than ever.

As for Finley, he understood that the cup he dreaded had not been one of destruction, but one of transformation. His faith in the Earth Mother and in his community was stronger than ever.

And so, Finley continued to listen to the Whispers of the Wind, always trusting that even in the most difficult times, there is a greater plan at work. And he often repeated those wise words to anyone who would listen:

"Abba, Father, everything is possible for you. Take this cup from me. Yet not what I will, but what you will."

"Abba, Father, everything is possible for you. Take this cup from me. Yet not what I will, but what you will."

Angel's Landing and the Forever Friends

IN THE QUAINT VILLAGE of Angel's Landing, people had a unique tradition. They believed that love is eternal, but the concept of marriage only belonged to the Earth. In their folklore, they often spoke about a day when they would rise to the heavens and become like the angels.

This tale was particularly fascinating to two young best friends, Amelia and Theo. They had known each other since they were toddlers and had always been inseparable.

Amelia and Theo would spend hours talking about what it'd be like to become angels. Theo would often say, "When we're angels, we won't need to get married to show we love each other. Our friendship will be forever!"

Amelia would smile and reply, "Exactly! Friendship is love, and love is eternal. It's like the wise words say, 'When the dead rise, they will neither marry nor be given in marriage; they will be like the angels in heaven.'"

As the years went by, Amelia and Theo grew older but their friendship remained unbreakable. They supported each other through hardships, celebrated victories, and always reminded one another of the sacred folklore of Angel's Landing.

One fateful day, a massive flood threatened the village. Amelia and Theo joined the rescue teams, helping to move people to higher ground. They worked tirelessly, and as the water began to recede, they found themselves atop the village's highest hill, where they had moved the last of the villagers to safety.

Exhausted but relieved, they looked at each other and smiled. At that moment, an old villager approached them. She was known for her wisdom and spiritual insights.

"You two remind me of the angels in our folklore," she said, smiling warmly. "I have no doubt that one day, you'll be just like them in heaven—forever friends."

Amelia and Theo looked at each other, their eyes filled with tears of joy and gratitude. They realized that their friendship was not just a worldly bond but a divine connection, one that would continue even in the heavens.

They hugged each other tightly and then joined hands, looking at the clearing skies above. And as they stood there, their hearts full of love and their souls filled with the promise of eternal friendship, they whispered the sacred words:

"When the dead rise, they will neither marry nor be given in marriage; they will be like the angels in heaven."

"When the dead rise, they will neither marry nor be given in marriage; they will be like the angels in heaven."

Timmy and the Day of the Celestial King

IN THE HUMBLE VILLAGE of Duskwood, where the sky was often a mix of orange and purple as if perpetually stuck between sunset and twilight, lived a young boy named Timmy. Timmy was unlike any other child in the village, fascinated not by games or toys, but by the sky.

He spent hours every day gazing at the clouds, drawing various shapes and figures he imagined could exist beyond the veil of the sky. Timmy often talked about the 'Celestial King,' a powerful and glorious figure he believed would one day visit the Earth. However, his claims were often met with laughter and ridicule.

"Ah, Timmy," chuckled Old Man Jenkins, "Always with your head in the clouds. You should focus more on what's down here."

Timmy would smile politely but held onto his belief. "The Celestial King will come one day, and then you'll see. He will come in clouds with great power and glory."

One afternoon, as Timmy was sketching cloud patterns by the riverside, he noticed the sky transforming. The usual orange and purple hues gave way to a shimmering gold, and the clouds began to gather in a peculiar formation.

"It's happening," Timmy whispered to himself.

Just then, the villagers felt a strange but pleasant energy engulf the land. They looked up and saw a dazzling figure descending from the clouds. It was as if the sky had opened up to welcome a king, a Celestial King.

The figure was majestic, emitting an ethereal glow, and its presence alone seemed to cleanse the very air. It touched down gently in the center of the village square.

"I am the Celestial King," the figure announced, his voice like melodious thunder. "I have come to remind you of the wonders beyond your sky, of the importance of faith and imagination. Those who dream and believe make the world a place of endless possibilities."

The villagers stood in awe, their skepticism vanishing in an instant.

Timmy walked up to the Celestial King, his eyes filled with tears of joy. "I knew you would come. I always believed."

The Celestial King smiled at Timmy. "And it is that belief that has the power to bring even a king from the clouds. Always hold onto it, young dreamer."

With that, the Celestial King ascended back into the sky, leaving a trail of shimmering stardust behind. The sky returned to its usual colors, but something had fundamentally changed in the hearts of the Duskwood villagers.

From that day on, nobody doubted Timmy or the extraordinary wonders beyond their sky. Whenever someone would gaze upwards, they would remember the day the Celestial King visited, and they'd think:

"At that time men will see the Son of Man coming in clouds with great power and glory."

The Parable of the Humble King

ONCE UPON A TIME, IN a small village called Harmony, lived a humble boy named Leo. Despite being poor, he was known for his radiant smile and kindness. Leo had a unique way of seeing the world; he believed that even the smallest act of love could bring great joy.

One day, an old beggar named Mabel came to the village. Her clothes were tattered, and she carried a bag filled with nothing but a loaf of bread and some dried herbs. The villagers didn't pay much attention to her, busy with their own lives. However, Leo approached Mabel with a warm smile.

"Welcome to Harmony, would you like some fresh water?" he offered.

Mabel was touched. "You are kind, young man. Most people avoid me."

"Blessed are you who are poor, for yours is the kingdom of God," said Leo softly. "I believe that everyone has something valuable to offer."

Intrigued, Mabel handed Leo her loaf of bread. "Please, divide this bread among those who need it. Maybe then, they'll understand the kingdom you speak of."

Leo accepted the bread and did just that. He shared it with the sick, the old, and even the grumpy Mr. Thompson who never smiled.

Days passed, and Mabel's visit became a distant memory. However, something had changed in Harmony. People started to greet each other warmly and share what they had, be it a kind word, a loaf of bread, or a helping hand.

Soon, the village was full of laughter and happiness. It seemed as though a sense of unity had descended upon Harmony, and everyone felt it—even Mr. Thompson smiled.

On a bright day, when the sun was at its peak, a radiant figure appeared in the center of the village. It was Mabel, but she was no longer an old beggar. Her clothes shone like gold, and her face was glowing.

"I am the Guardian of Compassion, sent from the kingdom of God," she announced. "Leo, your kindness and wisdom have shown the people of Harmony what it means to be truly rich. You've taught them that the kingdom of God is not about gold or silver, but love and compassion."

As a token of gratitude, Mabel touched Leo's heart, and it glowed with a golden light. "Carry this light within you, and share it with the world."

Mabel vanished, leaving the villagers in awe. But the golden light remained in Leo's heart, reminding everyone in Harmony that the real treasure lay not in material wealth but in the love they shared.

From then on, Leo lived by the words, "Blessed are you who are poor, for yours is the kingdom of God," and Harmony became a village where everyone—rich or poor—felt like they belonged to a heavenly kingdom.

"Blessed are you who are poor, for yours is the kingdom of God."

The Parable of the Hungry Bunny

ONCE UPON A TIME, IN the cozy meadows of GreenValley, lived a small bunny named Ben. Ben was different from the other bunnies in one particular way: he was always hungry—not for food, but for knowledge.

While the other bunnies were content munching on carrots and hopping around, Ben always had his tiny nose buried in books or in conversations with the wise Elder Owl who lived in the oldest tree of the forest.

"Isn't it boring to read and learn all day?" his friend Luna would ask him.

"No," Ben would say with twinkling eyes, "every page I read and every word from Elder Owl fills me up like the juiciest of carrots."

One day, the peaceful GreenValley was threatened by a mysterious fog that made all the vegetation wither. The animals were worried and didn't know what to do. Luna, who loved her daily munch on fresh green grass, was particularly sad.

Seeing the distress in his community, Ben remembered a lesson from Elder Owl about ancient herbs that could replenish the soil. The only problem was that these herbs were located beyond the treacherous Dark Forest.

Undeterred, Ben announced, "I may be small, but I have learned much. I will go and find the magical herbs to save GreenValley!"

Though his journey was filled with challenges—crossing rivers, avoiding predators, and navigating through the maze-like forest—Ben's hunger for knowledge had prepared him for this.

Finally, he reached the Clearing of Wishes where the magical herbs grew. With a grateful heart, he picked the herbs and hurried back.

When he returned and the herbs were planted, the fog lifted. Slowly but surely, GreenValley returned to its original splendor. The animals cheered and danced, their hearts full of joy and their bellies soon to be full of fresh vegetation.

Elder Owl spoke, "Today, we witnessed the power of knowledge and the courage of a small bunny. Ben, blessed are you who hunger now, for you are satisfied—and so is the entire GreenValley."

From that day on, the animals started visiting Elder Owl and reading more, their hunger for knowledge ignited by Ben's courageous act. And as for Ben, his appetite for learning never ceased, for he knew that the best satisfaction came from a hunger for wisdom and kindness.

"Blessed are you who hunger now, for you will be satisfied."

Sad Sally and the Magical Meadow

IN THE ANIMAL KINGDOM of Joyful Grove, everyone seemed happy and content—everyone except for Sad Sally, a young turtle who always seemed to have a gloomy cloud hovering over her shell. While other animals played and laughed, Sally would often be found weeping near the Lonely Pond.

"Why are you always so sad, Sally?" asked Jolly Rabbit, who couldn't understand why anyone would choose to be unhappy in such a delightful place.

"I don't know," sighed Sally. "Sometimes I feel overwhelmed, like I carry the weight of the world on my shell."

Many animals tried to cheer her up—Jolly Rabbit told jokes, Happy Hedgehog sang songs, and even Wise Owl shared some uplifting words. But the cloud over Sally's shell wouldn't go away.

One day, a mysterious hummingbird named Harmony visited Joyful Grove. Harmony was magical and had the power to see the hidden feelings of creatures. As soon as she saw Sally, she knew that this young turtle had a special role to play.

Harmony took Sally to a hidden meadow, known only to her. This meadow was full of flowers that bloomed once in a lifetime—the Tears-to-Laughter Lilies.

"Blessed are you who weep now, for you will laugh," said Harmony, touching a flower with her beak. The flower turned into a radiant gem, emitting a light that instantly made Sally feel a little lighter.

"How do you feel?" asked Harmony.

"I feel... better, like some of the weight has lifted," replied Sally, surprised by the sudden change.

"These are no ordinary flowers," said Harmony. "They bloom from the tears of those who truly feel, and in return, they give the gift of lightness and laughter. Your tears have nourished these blooms."

Harmony gave Sally a small pouch of the radiant gems to take back with her. "Share these with those who need it, and remember, your capacity to feel deeply is not a curse, but a gift."

Returning to Joyful Grove, Sally distributed the radiant gems to other animals. To everyone's surprise, even those who seemed forever joyful had moments of hidden sadness, and the gems made them feel lighter too.

As for Sad Sally, the cloud over her shell slowly lifted. While she still had her moments, she also found herself laughing more often, truly cherishing the joy because she knew the depths of sadness.

And so, Joyful Grove became a place not just of perpetual happiness, but of authentic emotion, where every tear and every laugh had its own unique value.

"Blessed are you who weep now, for you will laugh."

Brave Benny and the Mysterious Island

IN THE TRANQUIL WATERS of Faithful Bay, there lived a young fish named Brave Benny. Despite his name, Benny wasn't particularly brave; in fact, he was terrified of venturing beyond the safety of the coral reef where he and his friends played.

One fine day, Benny's pals dared him to explore the Mysterious Island, a place no fish from Faithful Bay had ever returned from. Trembling fin to fin, Benny was filled with apprehension but didn't want to let his friends down.

He thought of what his Grandma Gilly used to tell him, "Courage isn't the absence of fear, Benny. It's doing something despite being afraid."

Taking a deep gulp of water, Benny began his journey towards the Mysterious Island. As he swam closer, a sudden storm swept the sea, filling it with crashing waves and roaring winds. Benny wanted to turn back but remembered Grandma Gilly's words.

Suddenly, he saw a glowing figure moving gracefully in the water. The figure came closer and revealed itself to be a majestic sea turtle named Tranquil Tina.

"Take courage! It is I. Don't be afraid," Tina said in a soothing voice. Her calm presence had a magical effect on Benny, who felt his fears wash away.

With Tina leading the way, they reached the Mysterious Island, which was not as frightening as the legends had claimed. In fact, it was a haven full of vibrant corals and playful sea creatures. Benny realized that the island had only remained mysterious because no one had the courage to explore it.

Encouraged and emboldened, Benny returned to Faithful Bay with Tranquil Tina by his side. The other fish were astonished to see him return, and even more surprised when they heard about the wonders of the Mysterious Island.

Benny became a hero, not because he was fearless, but because he had faced his fears. From that day on, he was truly deserving of his name, Brave Benny, and Faithful Bay had one more story of courage to pass on to future generations.

"Take courage! It is I. Don't be afraid."

Friendly Fred and the Judging Jester

ONCE UPON A TIME, IN the cheerful town of Wisdomville, lived a boy named Friendly Fred. Fred was a considerate and caring young man, always ready to lend a hand or offer a kind word. He held a simple yet powerful philosophy close to his heart: "Do not judge and you will not be judged. Do not condemn, and you will not be condemned. Forgive and you will be forgiven."

Fred was friends with everyone in Wisdomville, except for the Judging Jester. The Jester loved nothing more than poking fun at people, often making them feel small or inadequate. He had a knack for judging others without understanding their struggles or dreams.

One sunny afternoon, the Jester decided to make fun of old Mr. Wiggins, the town's blacksmith. Mr. Wiggins had always been a bit clumsy and was known for occasionally burning himself while working. The Jester made a cruel joke about Mr. Wiggins being so clumsy that he couldn't even forge a simple nail without getting burned.

Fred, who happened to hear the jest, took the Jester aside. "Why do you enjoy making people feel bad about themselves? What if someone judged you for every mistake you've made?"

The Jester scoffed. "Oh, come on, Fred. It's all in good fun."

A few days later, the Jester found himself in a predicament. While performing a juggling act, he dropped his balls in front of the whole town. The crowd giggled and some even jeered, but Fred walked up to the Jester and helped him pick up the juggling balls.

"Why are you helping me?" The Jester was puzzled.

Fred smiled, "Do not judge and you will not be judged. Do not condemn, and you will not be condemned. Forgive and you will be forgiven."

The Jester was stunned. Despite his previous actions, Fred had shown him kindness and understanding. That simple act of forgiveness and non-judgment made the Jester reevaluate his own behavior.

From that day on, the Judging Jester transformed. He still performed and made people laugh, but his humor was no longer at the expense of others. He had learned the importance of not judging or condemning people, and how good it felt to be forgiven.

As for Friendly Fred, he continued to live his life with a heart full of compassion, never judging, always forgiving. And so, both boys grew up to be wise and generous men, all because they embraced the lesson: "Do not judge and you will not be judged. Do not condemn, and you will not be condemned. Forgive and you will be forgiven."

"Do not judge and you will not be judged. Do not condemn, and you will not be condemned. Forgive and you will be forgiven."

Two Wells

ONCE UPON A TIME IN the mystical land of Virtuoso, two wells stood side by side, known as the Wells of Essence. These were no ordinary wells; they had the unique ability to reflect the true nature of anyone who came to draw water from them. One well was called GoodHeart, and the other was named DarkSoul.

GoodHeart was frequented by Gracious Graham, a farmer known throughout Virtuoso for his kindness and altruism. On the other hand, the somber and mistrustful Vile Victor often drew water from DarkSoul. Both men believed in an old adage: "The good man brings good things out of the good stored up in his heart, and the evil man brings evil things out of the evil stored up in his heart. For out of the overflow of his heart, his mouth speaks."

Gracious Graham, when drawing water from GoodHeart, would often find that the well overflowed with the purest water that nurtured his crops, making them flourish like never before. When he spoke, his words carried wisdom and kindness, affecting everyone he met in a positive way. His crops were healthy, his farm animals thrived, and people from all walks of life respected and loved him.

Vile Victor, however, had a very different experience with DarkSoul. Whenever he drew water, it was always just enough, but tainted, cloudy, and unrefreshing. His words were often bitter, and his actions were malevolent. Consequently, his crops withered, his farm animals were restless, and the people of Virtuoso avoided him.

One fateful day, Virtuoso was hit by a severe drought. The rivers dried up, and the earth cracked. Desperate, both men went to their respective wells. This time, GoodHeart's water seemed even purer, as if blessing Graham for his consistent goodness. DarkSoul, however, was nearly empty, offering just a sludgy mess to Victor.

The villagers, running out of options, heard about the Wells of Essence and decided to see if they could find some relief. When they tasted the water from GoodHeart, it was like a miracle; their energy was restored, and hope surged through their veins. Gracious Graham gladly shared not only the water but also the abundant crops that he had nurtured through it.

No one dared to try the water from DarkSoul, knowing well the kind of man Vile Victor was. In a moment of realization, Victor felt the weight of his choices and looked longingly at GoodHeart.

"Would you like to try drawing water from GoodHeart?" Graham asked, breaking the silence.

"Will it allow me?" Victor questioned, skeptical yet curious.

"GoodHeart reflects what's inside you. Perhaps it's time to consider what you're storing up in your heart," Graham advised, recalling the proverb that had guided his actions for years.

And so, with hesitation, Victor took a step towards change. As he drew water from GoodHeart, he was surprised to find it neither pure nor tainted but somewhat cloudy—a reflection of his newfound intention to change.

From that day on, Vile Victor transformed, taking to heart the lesson of the Wells of Essence. His actions began to align with good, and over time, the water he drew from GoodHeart became clearer.

As for Gracious Graham, he continued to be a beacon of goodness, living by the axiom, "The good man brings good things out of the good stored up in his heart, and the evil man brings evil things out of the evil stored up in his heart. For out of the overflow of his heart, his mouth speaks."

Thus, Virtuoso became a land where every heart strived for purity, understanding that their essence influenced not just their own lives, but the wellbeing of all.

"The good man brings good things out of the good stored up in his heart, and the evil man brings evil things out of the evil stored up in his heart. For out of the overflow of his heart his mouth speaks."

The Orchard of Wisdom

ONCE UPON A TIME IN a tranquil village named Harmonsville, a wise old man named Elder Ethan had an enchanting orchard full of diverse fruit trees. However, this was no ordinary orchard; it was known as the Orchard of Wisdom. It was said that the fruits of these trees had the ability to imbue people with incredible wisdom and clarity of thought, but only if they were used properly.

Elder Ethan had three sons—Paul, Peter, and Patrick—who helped him take care of the orchard. Though they were all trained in the same traditions, their approaches were quite different.

Paul listened to his father's teachings and believed them wholeheartedly but never put them into practice. He was content with merely knowing what should be done but never actually doing it.

Peter, on the other hand, heard his father's teachings but always questioned them. He thought he knew better and would often tweak the formulas and ignore the traditional ways of nurturing the orchard.

Lastly, there was Patrick, who not only listened attentively to his father's words but also took great care in applying them. He understood that wisdom was both in listening and in practicing.

One summer, a terrible blight struck the region. Many farms and orchards were affected, and the villagers were in despair. Elder Ethan gathered his sons and told them, "My mother and brothers are those who hear God's word and put it into practice. This orchard, too, will only thrive if its caretakers both hear and practice wisdom."

Paul did nothing, believing that if it was meant to be, the trees would heal themselves. Peter tried his own methods, disregarding his father's instructions. Patrick, however, diligently followed his father's traditional methods, which involved using a special blend of natural fertilizers and prayers.

After some weeks, the results were astonishing. The trees under Patrick's care not only survived but thrived, bearing the juiciest and most flavorful fruits. Paul's trees had succumbed to the blight, and Peter's had barely made it but bore no fruits.

Elder Ethan looked at his sons and the state of their respective trees. "You see," he said, "knowledge is but the beginning of wisdom. True wisdom blossoms only when you put into practice what you've learned."

The villagers benefited immensely from Patrick's fruits, gaining wisdom and insights they had never known before. Paul and Peter realized the importance of practicing what they had learned and vowed to follow their father's teachings henceforth.

And so, it was understood in Harmonsville that wisdom was not just in hearing but in doing, aligning with Elder Ethan's belief that his true kin were those who practiced what they heard, just like his most dutiful son, Patrick.

"My mother and brothers are those who hear God's word and put it into practice."

The Wise Elephant and the Echoing Jungle

IN A LUSH JUNGLE FILLED with chattering monkeys, fluttering butterflies, and glistening streams, there lived an old and wise elephant named Ella. Ella was the elder of the jungle and known for her wisdom. All the animals looked up to her and often sought her advice.

Ella had a young apprentice named Timmy the Turtle. Timmy wasn't the fastest or the strongest in the jungle, but he was a great listener, and he loved learning from Ella.

One day, Ella told Timmy, "You have learned much, young Timmy. Now it's your turn to share wisdom with others. Remember, he who listens to you, listens to me; he who rejects you, rejects me; but he who rejects me, rejects the wisdom of the jungle itself."

Timmy felt a bit overwhelmed but also excited. He had never spoken to the other animals on his own before. Taking a deep breath, he slowly began his journey across the jungle to share the wisdom Ella had taught him.

First, he met Benny the Butterfly, who was having a hard time choosing which flower to land on. Timmy advised Benny to choose flowers that not only looked pretty but also smelled good, for that would be good for both him and the flower. Benny listened and thanked Timmy.

Next, Timmy encountered Monica the Monkey, who was too afraid to swing to a higher branch to reach a ripe banana. Timmy encouraged her to face her fears and also to use her tail as an extra grip. Monica followed the advice and successfully reached her prize.

But then Timmy met Randy the Rhino, who was frustrated because he kept missing when he tried to charge at a coconut to break it open. Timmy suggested that Randy should take a few steps back to gain a better perspective before charging. Randy scoffed and ignored Timmy's advice, missing the coconut once again.

Feeling a bit discouraged, Timmy returned to Ella and shared his experiences. Ella chuckled softly, "You did well, young Timmy. Those who listened to your wisdom listened to me, and they gained from it. Randy, who rejected your counsel, not only rejected you and me but also the wisdom of the jungle itself."

Timmy understood, and from that day on, he was never afraid to share the wisdom Ella had imparted to him. And the animals, young and old, realized that wisdom could come from the most unexpected places—or creatures—as long as they were willing to listen.

"He who listens to you listens to me; he who rejects you rejects me; but he who rejects me rejects him who sent me."

The Prayer Tree

ONCE UPON A TIME, IN a magical forest, there stood an ancient tree known to all as the Prayer Tree. It was no ordinary tree; its leaves had a silvery shimmer, and its branches seemed to touch the sky.

In this forest lived a young rabbit named Riley. He had heard stories of the Prayer Tree, but he had never actually seen it. One day, after experiencing a particularly rough day where he argued with his friends and felt lost, Riley decided to search for the Prayer Tree.

After hopping through thickets and over streams, he finally arrived. The tree was even more magnificent than he had imagined.

Taking a deep breath, Riley stood under the tree and spoke the words he had learned from Grandma Whiskers, "Father, hallowed be your name, your kingdom come. Give us each day our daily bread. Forgive us our sins, for we also forgive everyone who sins against us. And lead us not into temptation."

As Riley said each word, the Prayer Tree's leaves glowed brighter. When he was done, a gentle wind blew, and a silver leaf floated down, landing softly in his paws.

Suddenly, Riley felt lighter. His worries seemed to disappear, and he felt a strange warmth in his heart.

As he hopped back home, he realized something miraculous: his friends greeted him with smiles, and the grudges they had held seemed to be forgotten.

From then on, whenever Riley or any of the forest animals were in need of guidance or peace, they would visit the Prayer Tree and recite the special prayer. And each time, the forest became a happier, more peaceful place for everyone.

So, remember, little ones, in times of worry, strife, or need, saying a prayer from the heart can bring peace and love like the magical leaves of the Prayer Tree.

"When you pray say: Father, hallowed be your name, your kingdom come. Give us each day our daily bread. Forgive us our sins, for we also forgive everyone who sins against us. And lead us not into temptation."

Sparrow's Special Day

IN THE SUNNY MEADOWS of GreenValley, life was peaceful for all the animals. Among them was a little sparrow named Sparky. Sparky was always cheerful but sometimes felt a little insignificant. He would often watch as animals like deer and rabbits got lots of attention from people who visited the meadow.

"They're so big and colorful," Sparky sighed to himself. "No one would notice if a tiny sparrow like me wasn't around."

One day, Sparky's friend Daisy the butterfly fluttered by. "What's wrong, Sparky? You look so glum!"

"I'm just a sparrow, Daisy. There are so many of us, and we all look the same. I feel like I don't matter," Sparky chirped sadly.

Daisy fluttered her wings thoughtfully. "You might feel small, Sparky, but you're special in your own way."

Just then, Old Owl, the wisest creature in GreenValley, landed on a branch nearby. "Ah, feeling a little down, are we? Let me tell you a secret, young Sparky. Do you know that not a single creature in this valley is forgotten? You may feel unimportant, but every hair on your head is special, every feather in your wings is unique. You're worth more than you think."

Sparky looked up, his eyes shining with hope. "Really, Old Owl? Do you really think so?"

Old Owl nodded wisely. "Indeed. You see, we're all part of this grand tapestry of life. Each of us, no matter how small, has a role to play. Are not five sparrows sold for just two pennies in the market? Yet, each of you is unforgettable. Don't be afraid; you're worth more than many sparrows."

Sparky's heart felt lighter, and he chirped a cheerful tune. The news that he was special and unique made him happier than he had been in a long time. From that day on, Sparky sang louder and flew higher, knowing that he was a valued part of the world around him.

And so, Sparky learned that no matter how ordinary he felt, he was extraordinary in his own way—never to be forgotten but forever cherished.

"Are not five sparrows sold for two pennies? Yet not one of them is forgotten by God. Indeed, the very hairs of your head are all numbered. Don't be afraid; you are worth more than many sparrows."

Timmy's Lesson in Greed

ONCE UPON A TIME IN the peaceful town of SweetVale, lived a young raccoon named Timmy. Timmy had a love for shiny things. Whether it was a glittering pebble or a sparkling button, Timmy wanted it all.

But Timmy wasn't happy. Even with all his shiny treasures, something felt missing.

One day, Wise Walter, the elder turtle of the town, decided to hold a gathering. "My dear friends," he began, "I have a magical acorn, one that gleams like a thousand sunsets. I will give it to the one who truly needs it."

Hearing this, Timmy's eyes sparkled. "A magical acorn that gleams? Oh, that should be mine!" he thought.

When the gathering ended, Timmy rushed up to Wise Walter. "Oh, Wise Walter, I need that magical acorn. With it, my collection would be complete!"

Wise Walter looked down at Timmy and sighed, "Is your happiness really built on shiny objects, Timmy?"

"Of course! The more I have, the happier I get!" Timmy exclaimed.

Wise Walter shook his head, "Watch out, young Timmy! Be on your guard against all kinds of greed; a raccoon's life does not consist of the abundance of his possessions."

Confused, Timmy went home but couldn't stop thinking about Wise Walter's words.

The next day, Timmy saw Little Lily, a young squirrel who was sad because she had nothing to play with. Remembering Wise Walter's words, Timmy gave Lily a shiny pebble from his collection.

The joy in Little Lily's eyes made Timmy feel a happiness he'd never felt before. At that moment, he realized that the true treasures in life were not things, but the happiness and well-being of those around him.

From then on, Timmy didn't collect shiny objects to keep but shared them with others who needed a little sparkle in their lives. And in doing so, he found the real magic was not in possessions but in generosity and love.

And Wise Walter's magical acorn? Well, it found a home with someone who needed it, but Timmy learned he had something even more magical— a kind and generous heart.

"Watch out! Be on your guard against all kinds of greed; a man's life does not consist of the abundance of his possessions."

The Unclimbable Mountain and Timmy the Turtle

IN THE VIBRANT LAND of Wonderwood, where the trees whispered secrets and the rivers sang sweet lullabies, there was an enormous mountain called Skyreach that no creature had ever climbed.

Many brave adventurers, from Randy the Rabbit to Barry the Bear, tried and tried but couldn't get past the jagged rocks and swirling winds. "It's impossible!" they all said.

In Wonderwood, lived a tiny turtle named Timmy who always dreamed of reaching the top of Skyreach Mountain to see the stars up close. "I'm going to climb Skyreach and touch the stars," Timmy told his friends. But they all laughed, "Timmy, if the strongest and the fastest can't do it, what makes you think you can?"

Timmy was a believer. "What's impossible for others may be possible with a little help from above," he said, pointing his little turtle finger toward the sky.

Undeterred, Timmy started his slow, patient journey up the mountain. When he reached the jagged rocks that had stopped so many before him, he took a deep breath and whispered, "Help me accomplish the impossible."

Suddenly, a gust of gentle wind came, lifting him over the jagged rocks. When he got to the swirling winds, a warm, calming breeze blew, clearing his way. Timmy couldn't believe it. He was at the top!

From the peak of Skyreach, Timmy looked up and saw the stars twinkling like diamonds. He felt a warm glow around him, realizing that he had done what was said to be impossible.

Timmy returned to Wonderwood a hero, not because he was the strongest or the fastest, but because he had faith that anything was possible. And so, every animal in Wonderwood learned that while some things may seem impossible, with a little faith and help from above, miracles can happen.

"What is impossible with men is possible with God."

Benny the Butterfly's Second Chance

ONCE UPON A TIME, IN a bustling forest, lived Benny the Caterpillar. Benny was known for his vibrant colors and his knack for telling stories. Yet, Benny was troubled. He was getting older, and he was not as lively as he used to be.

"What's wrong, Benny?" asked Dolly the Dove.

"I feel like I've missed something important in life," sighed Benny, "and I don't know what it is."

Just then, Grandpa Oak, the wisest tree in the forest, overheard Benny. "Ah, Benny," he rustled his leaves, "you're ready for your great transformation. You see, no one can truly understand the splendors of life unless they are born again."

Confused but intrigued, Benny asked, "Born again? How can that be?"

Grandpa Oak pointed to a secluded branch. "Go there, build your cocoon, and you'll understand."

Taking Grandpa Oak's advice to heart, Benny built a cocoon on the secluded branch. For days, he remained inside, transforming. It was a challenging process. There were moments of doubt and discomfort, but Benny persevered, holding onto the hope of discovering something magnificent.

On the seventh day, Benny felt a new energy surging through him. He burst out of his cocoon and fluttered his new, beautiful wings. Benny was no longer a caterpillar; he was a magnificent butterfly!

As he flew around, Benny realized he saw the world differently. He could now reach heights he had never imagined and see the beauty of the forest from above. The colors were more vivid, the scents more fragrant, and he felt an overwhelming sense of peace and happiness.

He returned to his friends, who were amazed at his transformation. "I was born again," Benny explained, "and now I understand the true splendor of life. It's as if I'm seeing the world for the very first time!"

Dolly the Dove was in awe. "You're a living testament that it's never too late for a fresh start," she cooed.

From then on, Benny the Butterfly became the symbol of hope and renewal in the forest. He shared his story far and wide, inspiring other animals to seek their own transformations and to be 'born again' in their own unique ways.

And so, the animals in the forest lived their lives, always conscious of the transformative power of renewal and the wisdom that comes with new beginnings.

"I tell you the truth, no one can see the kingdom of God unless he is born again."

Timmy Turtle's Wishful Stone

ONCE UPON A TIME, IN Whispering Pond, lived Timmy Turtle. Timmy was a friendly little turtle with a big imagination. He had many friends, but he always felt like he wasn't fast enough to play some of the games his friends loved. "Oh, how I wish I could be as quick as Freddie the Frog," he often thought.

One day, Timmy stumbled upon an unusual, glittering stone at the edge of the pond. Lizzie the Ladybug, the wisest insect in the pond, fluttered by and noticed Timmy examining the stone.

"That, dear Timmy, is the Wishful Stone. Legend has it that if you truly believe, the stone will grant you a single wish," said Lizzie.

Timmy's eyes widened. A single wish? The possibilities raced through his mind, but he knew exactly what he wanted.

Closing his eyes tightly, Timmy held the Wishful Stone and wished, "I wish I could be as fast as Freddie the Frog. Oh, I believe I can be, I truly do!"

Lizzie smiled, "You must hold onto that belief, Timmy, even when you don't see immediate results."

Weeks passed, and Timmy didn't notice any change. But he practiced every day, swimming through the pond, believing in his wish. He never let go of his belief, always carrying the Wishful Stone with him.

Then, one sunny afternoon, the animals organized a race. Timmy hesitated but then remembered the Wishful Stone and his wish. "I believe," he whispered to himself.

As the race started, Timmy felt an incredible surge of energy. His flippers paddled faster than ever, and to everyone's surprise, he kept pace with Freddie the Frog, eventually crossing the finish line at the same time as him!

Cheers erupted from the crowd. Timmy couldn't believe it; his wish had come true because he had believed in it all along.

Lizzie flew up to him and said, "See, believing made it real. Your wish was granted because you held onto your faith."

From that day on, Timmy became an inspiration to all the animals in Whispering Pond. They learned that sometimes wishes do come true, but only if you believe in them wholeheartedly.

And so, Timmy Turtle lived happily, always cherishing his Wishful Stone, a symbol of the incredible power of belief and the wonders that can be achieved through faith.

"Therefore I tell you, whatever you ask for in prayer, believe that you have received it, and it will be yours."

The Brave Firefly of Truth Forest

IN THE MAGICAL TRUTH Forest, a small but courageous firefly named Sparkle had a unique gift. Unlike other fireflies, Sparkle's light was extra bright and warm, casting away darkness wherever she flew.

Many animals in the forest liked to play hide-and-seek, and sometimes they even told little fibs or hid things from each other. But Sparkle was different; she loved the truth. She believed that honesty was like her light, warming everyone it touched.

One evening, a troubling rumor swept through the forest. Someone was stealing the fruits from the community orchard. Animals became suspicious and started blaming each other. The atmosphere grew cold and dark, just like a night without stars.

The Wise Old Owl called for a meeting at the heart of the forest. "Friends," he began, "there is an easy way to solve this mystery. We should all tell the truth."

The animals were silent. Many were afraid to speak because they thought others might not believe them. That's when Sparkle flew into the center of the gathering, her light shining brighter than ever.

"Dear friends," said Sparkle, "I believe in the truth, and so my light will shine on whoever tells it. Don't be afraid; the truth will set us free."

Sparkle's warm light filled the clearing, touching each animal softly. Encouraged by her bravery, one by one, they started sharing what they knew. Finally, Rascal the raccoon admitted that he was the one who had been taking the fruits.

"I'm sorry," Rascal said, his eyes meeting Sparkle's light. "I didn't know how to ask, and I was afraid you'd say no."

Wise Old Owl looked at Sparkle and smiled, "Your light, dear Sparkle, has shown us all the power of the truth. When we are honest, our actions are like a bright light that can guide others."

From that day on, all the animals of Truth Forest knew that honesty was more than a word; it was a way to live by. And Sparkle, the brave firefly, kept shining her light, reminding everyone that truth is the path that leads us into the light.

"But whoever lives by the truth comes into the light, so that it may be seen plainly that what he has done has been done through God."

The Never-Ending Work of Father Sky and Little Cloud

IN THE VAST, ENDLESS sky lived Father Sky and his little helper, Little Cloud. They were always busy creating beautiful days and starry nights for everyone who lived on the land below. The animals, the trees, and the humans looked up to admire their creations and felt grateful for the sunny days and gentle rains.

Father Sky was always at work, painting the morning sun and weaving the fabric of the night. "I must never stop working, for the world depends on me," said Father Sky, his voice echoing like thunder.

Little Cloud loved helping his father but sometimes felt overwhelmed. "Father, don't you ever rest? The work never seems to end."

Father Sky chuckled, "My work is endless, Little Cloud, but it is also joyous. I find happiness in lighting up the world below and in seeing the flowers bloom and the children play. And you, too, have an important role. Your rain nurtures the fields, and your shade cools the Earth."

Feeling inspired, Little Cloud decided to work with renewed energy. He went down to provide some much-needed rain to the thirsty land. The rivers rejoiced, the plants perked up, and the animals danced in the gentle shower.

As Little Cloud returned to Father Sky, he felt a sense of fulfillment. "Father, now I understand why we must keep working. Our work is not just a duty; it's a gift that keeps the world turning."

Father Sky nodded with pride, "Exactly, Little Cloud. Our work is a never-ending cycle that brings life and joy to the world. And it's comforting to know that you'll be here to continue the work long after I'm gone."

Little Cloud felt grateful and motivated, floating higher and brighter than ever before, ready for the endless, rewarding work that lay ahead.

"My Father is always at his work to this very day, and I, too, am working."

The Bridge Between Two Worlds

IN THE LAND OF EVERGRAY, where the skies were always cloudy and the trees forever leafless, lived a young girl named Emily. She had always heard tales of a land called Foreverbright, where the sun always shone and flowers never ceased to bloom. But to reach Foreverbright, one had to cross an invisible bridge, a bridge that only appeared to those who believed in the wise words of Old Owl, the guardian of wisdom.

Old Owl was ancient and wise, and he lived atop the highest tree in Evergray. He had a message that he'd share with everyone: "Trust in the wisdom of the Great Spirit who created all lands, and you'll find the bridge that leads to Foreverbright."

Many people heard Old Owl's words but only a few truly listened. Emily was one of those who not only heard but believed. Fueled by her faith, she set off to find the elusive bridge.

Emily reached the spot where the bridge was said to exist. At first, she saw nothing but the endless abyss below. She took a deep breath, recalling Old Owl's wisdom. Trusting in the words of the wise owl and the Great Spirit, she took a courageous step forward.

To her amazement, her foot landed on something solid. The invisible bridge had become visible to her, and she had literally crossed over from the land of Evergray to Foreverbright.

When Emily set foot in Foreverbright, she found herself in a world full of color, light, and endless beauty. She realized that she had found something much greater than a physical place; she had discovered a realm of eternal joy, peace, and love.

Back in Evergray, Emily's story spread like wildfire. Those who heard and believed in Old Owl's words also found their way to Foreverbright. They realized that Emily had indeed crossed over from a life of perpetual gloom to one of eternal brightness, all because she listened and believed.

"I tell you the truth, whoever hears my word and believes him who sent me has eternal life and will not be condemned; he has crossed over from death to life."

The Light of Belief

AFTER THE FESTIVAL of Praises, Foreverbright was calm and serene. However, many creatures began to wonder what was next. "What is the work that we should now focus on?" they asked Old Owl.

Old Owl gathered everyone around the Wisdom Tree and spoke softly, "The true work of the Great Spirit is simple yet profound. We must believe in the light that has been sent to guide us."

Just then, a gentle beam of light emanated from the Wisdom Tree and pointed towards a distant mountain. "The Light of Belief," gasped Rosie Rabbit.

"We must follow it," announced Old Owl.

Emily, Rosie Rabbit, Leonard the Lion, and Tina the Bluebird set off on another journey. As they approached the mountain, the terrain became difficult, filled with obstacles and challenges. Yet, they all believed in the Light of Belief and pressed on.

When they reached the mountain's peak, they found a small, glowing orb. "This is the Light of Belief," said Old Owl, appearing beside them. "It remains constant, even when you can't see it. Your job is to carry this belief back to Foreverbright and share it with everyone."

Filled with awe, Emily gently picked up the Light of Belief and carried it back. Upon their return, every creature touched the light and felt a warm, calming energy fill their hearts.

From that day on, every being in Foreverbright understood that their main job was to believe in the goodness that the Great Spirit had sent their way. They realized that sometimes doing the work of the Great Spirit wasn't about doing at all—it was about believing.

And so, with hearts full of faith, the creatures of Foreverbright lived harmoniously, forever guided by the Light of Belief.

"The work of God is this: to believe in the one he has sent."

The Mystery of the Whispering Winds

NOT LONG AFTER OLD Owl had soared to the great beyond, strange whispers began to fill the air of Foreverbright. Rosie Rabbit, Leonard the Lion, Emily the Elephant, and the other creatures heard them as the winds blew through the Wisdom Tree.

"What are these whispers?" asked Leonard, his ears twitching in curiosity.

Emily's large ears also perked up, "They seem to be saying something important!"

They all huddled close to the Wisdom Tree, and as if in answer, its leaves rustled to form words, "The Spirit gives life; the body is only temporary. Listen to the words of the whispering winds, for they are spirit, and they bring life."

"Wow! What does that mean?" asked Rosie Rabbit, her eyes wide with wonder.

Old Turtle, who had been silent till now, spoke, "Ah, this means our life's essence isn't just our physical selves. Our spirits are what make us truly alive. The whispers are a reminder that the things of the spirit are life-giving."

Everyone thought about this deeply. They remembered Old Owl and the Light of Belief that had lifted him. Leonard said, "So, the Light of Belief was like a spirit, always giving us life even when our bodies grow old and weary."

"Exactly," said Old Turtle. "The spirit is eternal. When we focus on being kind, loving, and brave, we nourish our spirits, and we truly live. The whispering winds are a reminder to keep our spirits strong."

From that day on, whenever the whispering winds blew through Foreverbright, the creatures felt a new kind of joy. They knew they were more than their bodies; their spirits were eternal, nurtured by their beliefs, their love for one another, and the wisdom that flowed through the land.

The end... or perhaps, the continuation of many more adventures in spirit and in life.

Here, the focus is on the concept of the spirit as the true source of life, something that persists beyond physical existence. This tale could serve as a way to teach children about the importance of spiritual and emotional well-being, compassion, and the immaterial things that enrich life.

"The Spirit gives life; the flesh counts for nothing. The words I have spoken to you are spirit and they are life."

The New Dawn of Love in Foreverbright

AS THE GOLDEN DAYS turned into weeks, and weeks into months, Foreverbright was a happier place than ever before. Leonard the Lion felt a sense of contentment as he saw animals being kinder, sharing more, and helping each other.

But on one peaceful afternoon, he felt a strange tingling sensation, almost like a soft whisper in the wind. It was as if the very air was telling him something important: "Love each other as you have been loved."

Leonard knew he had a new message to share. The golden rule had brought harmony, but perhaps it was love that would bring eternal happiness. He felt this message so deeply that he knew he had to share it immediately.

Gathering the animals of Foreverbright around the Mound of Wisdom, Leonard took a deep breath. "Dear friends," he began. "I feel there is yet another layer to our happiness, another key to making Foreverbright glow even more."

"And what is that?" asked Tina the Tiger, her eyes shimmering in anticipation.

"It's love," Leonard said simply. "We must love each other as we have been loved. That's the kind of love that asks for nothing in return, the kind of love that celebrates the happiness of others as if it were our own."

Tina looked puzzled. "How do you love someone as you've been loved, Leonard?"

Leonard smiled. "Think about your mother's love, or the love of a dear friend. That's a love that doesn't count favors, a love that's there for you, no matter what. Can we love each other in that way? Imagine how incredible Foreverbright would be then!"

So a new dawn rose over Foreverbright, casting a warm, pink glow that reflected the newfound love among its inhabitants. Benny the Bunny started taking care of sick animals, giving them the best herbs from his little garden. Harriet the Hawk started teaching younger birds how to soar high yet stay grounded. And Tina the Tiger started sharing stories, the very essence of her being, with everyone.

In Foreverbright, the golden rule had laid the foundation, but it was love that built the castle. Each animal found ways to express their love for one another, in actions big and small, creating a never-ending cycle of goodwill and happiness.

And so, from that day on, Leonard would often say: "In Foreverbright, we not only shine with individual brightness, but we also glow with collective love. And that is the most beautiful glow of all."

The end... until another new dawn in a land filled with not just respect and kindness, but abounding with love.

"A new command I give you: Love one another. As I have loved you, so you must love one another."

The Never-Ending Light in Foreverbright

AS THE DAYS GREW LONGER and the sunsets painted the skies with shades of orange, pink, and purple, Leonard the Lion felt a deep peace wash over him. Once again, he sensed a whisper in the wind, a comforting thought that filled him with warmth: "And know that I am with you always; yes, to the end of time."

Leonard realized that the messages he had shared weren't just lessons to be learned and then forgotten. They were like seeds planted deep in the hearts of every animal in Foreverbright—seeds that would grow and flourish for generations to come.

Standing atop the Mound of Wisdom one last time, Leonard addressed the gathering animals. "Dear friends, as we continue to live by the golden rule and fill our lives with love, remember that the spirit of goodness is always with us. It will guide us, protect us, and light our path, today, tomorrow, and forever."

Mimi the Mouse timidly raised her paw and asked, "So, the happiness and love will never end, Leonard?"

Leonard smiled, his eyes twinkling like the first stars of the evening. "Exactly, Mimi. The love and kindness we've learned to share are eternal. They will stay in Foreverbright and in our hearts, from now to the end of time. Because goodness is like the light of the moon and stars; even when you can't see it, it's always there."

As the animals dispersed, their hearts filled with joy and gratitude, Leonard felt the last rays of the setting sun embrace him. He knew that the journey to make Foreverbright a haven of kindness and love was never-ending. But that was the beauty of it—the light of goodness was eternal, and it would shine in the hearts of all creatures, forevermore.

The end... or rather, the beginning of countless new days under the never-ending light of love and wisdom.

In this epilogue, children learn about the comforting idea that goodness, love, and wisdom are eternal forces. They are always there to guide us, no matter what challenges we may face, reinforcing the idea that the journey of learning and growing never truly ends.

"And know that I am with you always; yes, to the end of time."

Rhett and the Worrying Woods"

AFTER RHETT AND THE young animals returned from the Three Gates of Wisdom, they discovered that something was troubling the hearts of the animals in Heartshine. The animals were getting more and more anxious about the uncertainties of the future. The Worrying Woods had cast its shadow over the community, filling the animals with unease and doubt.

Rhett called everyone for a gathering near Leonard's Wisdom Tree, the old tree where Leonard used to share his teachings. Rhett climbed onto a stump and looked around at the anxious faces of the young and old.

"My friends, I know that the shadow of the Worrying Woods has made us all uneasy. But I have another treasure from Leonard's wisdom to share," Rhett said, opening the golden book of wisdom to a page that read: "Do not let your hearts be troubled. Trust in God; trust also in me."

Rhett looked into the eyes of each animal and continued, "It means we should not let our worries and fears control us. Instead, we should trust in the greater goodness that watches over us. Just as you trusted Leonard and now trust me, believe that there's a greater plan for all of us."

As Rhett spoke, a miraculous thing happened. The golden rays of the sun broke through the dark clouds that hovered above the Worrying Woods, and its shadow started to recede. The Wisdom Tree's leaves shimmered, and a sense of calm enveloped the land.

The animals felt a weight lift off their shoulders. Their hearts were no longer troubled, replaced with a newfound trust in the goodness of life and in the wisdom that Rhett and Leonard had brought into their lives.

"Thank you, Rhett," said Ginny the giraffe, "for reminding us to trust and not be consumed by our worries."

From that day on, the animals of Heartshine faced the uncertainties of life with courage and trust, knowing they were part of a greater plan that was both loving and wise.

They had not only found the wisdom of the Way, the Truth, and the Life but had also discovered the power of Trust. The wisdom in their hearts grew stronger, and they knew they could face anything that came their way.

The end... but also another new beginning, a life with less worry and more trust for every animal in Heartshine.

"Do not let your hearts be troubled. Trust in God; trust also in me."

Don't miss out!

Visit the website below and you can sign up to receive emails whenever Cort Curtis publishes a new book. There's no charge and no obligation.

https://books2read.com/r/B-A-VNBAB-CDSNC

BOOKS 2 READ

Connecting independent readers to independent writers.

Did you love *I Am a Child of God*? Then you should read *All You Need Is Love*[1] by Cort Curtis!

Dive into a world where music transforms into enchanting tales! Drawing inspiration from some of The Beatles' most iconic songs, "Songs to Stories" offers a unique spin, turning beloved lyrics into heartwarming children's tales. Each story has been crafted to capture the essence of the original song while introducing lovable characters and unforgettable adventures.

Inside this captivating collection, you'll find:
"The Red Scarf": A tale of a young girl's journey in finding the owner of a mysterious scarf, teaching us about kindness, mystery, and the sentimental value of objects."The Lonely Stone": A moving narrative that explores loneliness, hope, and the power of community."The Tale

1. https://books2read.com/u/3yQezn

2. https://books2read.com/u/3yQezn

of Bungalow Bill": An adventurous ride with Bungalow Bill as he learns about the consequences of his actions and the importance of respecting all living beings.

... and many more!

Perfect for children aged 5 to 9, this collection not only serves as a delightful bedtime companion but also introduces them to the legendary music of The Beatles in a fresh, imaginative way. Parents and grandparents who cherished the timeless tunes will find joy in sharing these stories, bridging the gap between generations.

Join us on a magical journey where melodies come to life, teaching timeless lessons and creating memories that will stay with your child forever. Let's come together, right now, over these enchanting tales!

Also by Cort Curtis

All You Need Is Love
I Am a Child of God

About the Author

I'm a storyteller who writes tales inspired by the brave people I meet in my job as a helper. I love sharing stories that help us understand our feelings and each other better. ❖❤❖

About the Publisher

I am an independent publisher who writes books on love and awareness.